The Vamp

Helena Filligher

Table of contents

CHAPTER 1-THE NEW FACE.. 3

CHAPTER 2-THE EXPERIENCE 9

CHAPTER 3-HUMAN AGAIN 17

CHAPTER 4 -ATTACK ON HOUND.................................... 23

CHAPTER 5 -THE ESCAPE... 29

CHAPTER 6-THE NEW WORLD 38

CHAPTER 7-MEETING THE HYBRIDS 48

CHAPTER 8 -LAURA'S NEW HOME?................................ 54

CHAPTER 9 -VAMPIRES SHIFT 65

CHAPTER 10 -FINDING THE LOST PACK........................ 75

CHAPTER 11-NEW FAMILY.. 83

CHAPTER 12-CAUGHT OFF GUARD 93

CHAPTER 13-VAMPIRE ON THE RUN 104

CHAPTER 14 -CAPTURED.. 117

Chapter 1-The New Face

The excitement was too overwhelming simply because the new attendant was cute.

I thought he was new simply because he wasn't familiar, never set my eyes on him before, and after eight years here, I had this confidence that I virtually knew everybody at treatment facility in Hound. Patients along with staff came and went to and fro, but sadly, as unexpected, the turnover and population was less. Those who always stood out are those new faces.

And sure *this* guy's face could stand out almost anywhere.

He had amber eyes covered by long, thick lashes. His attribute were even, dominated by a strong nose and full lips. But the most salient thing about him was his smile. It was spread on his lips like jam on bread and was damn contagious with every little crystal appearance of his big white teeth.

"Done?" he asked with great sense of humour in his tone.

I dipped my head into a nod as I tried desperately to wander my gaze away from him before he knew that I had been staring---- not that he didn't know that the past few minutes I had settled my caramel brown eyes on him, staring.

I set the fork down gently beside my plate, then pushed the styled tray across the table towards him.

"Thanks." He took it up, holding up the tray on one arm. He glanced down at it, "You seem to have enjoyed every taste of it. Is the food really good?"

The question rang a bell in my head, why was it that every time I felt I was getting the hang of living life in this dry to death facility, something pops out silencing those feelings and taunting me with the beauty of living a normal life outside the walls of the hound facility.

A life where a twenty-five-year-old could live, hanging out with friends and making the best of what life had to offer, according to what the novels attendant Sarah brought every Friday evening talked about.

The attendant, whose name tag read *Damon*, released a devastating smile and a blush graced my cheeks as I realized I'd zoned out.

"It's okay," I answered, forcing my tongue to form words. "The meals professor Greyson recommends are sure what every patient in the Houston facility would need. Less varieties."

"And you don't mind that?"

I shrugged, sitting back in my chair.

"It's not really a question of whether I mind or don't mind," I said. "Professor Greyson is doing all to keeping me alive, so I pretty much do what they tell me."

The attendant ran his free hand through his dark blond hair and with a serious expression on his face. "Huh. Makes sense, I guess. Well, I hope they at least have the decency to let you have dessert once in a while."

I smiled broadly. "Don't worry, they do."

He chuckled. The sound of it sparked a fire in my stomach creating a blush on my cheeks and I could guess he was flirting with me.

The thought of it created a cloud of doubts within. Why would a guy like him flirt with a girl like me? It wasn't like I was hideous or anything. The brown hair that fell to my back was chocolate in colour, and although I wasn't allowed to wear makeup—in case its components triggered a negative reaction— Dad assured me I didn't need it. He said my golden eyes and high cheekbones did all the work for me, and makeup would only get in the way of my natural beauty.

Still, I couldn't picture this guy having difficulty in finding a date out in the real world. Well, the closest thing to a date in the facility would be a trip to the cafeteria under the surveillance of a couple of lab techs.

Which was why I apparently knew dating was not the thing for me till my feet could step out of the Hound facility relieved of my disease. As professor Greyson never failed to inform me that my illness was long termed and one that needed full attention, he had faith in his knowledge of science that one day he'd cure me.

I appreciated that. I didn't want him offering platitudes. But even though he reminded me that my immune would fail me in the outside world, I fully doubted that. Well I had to.

"Well... I'll get going. Looks like you've got a whole lot on your mind."

The attendant graced me another smile as he walked out my room turning toward the door.

Damn it! I'd zoned out on him, what in the world was wrong with me, I'd left him to take a trip with my thoughts. It was not that I had planned it that way but there was something about him that had opened the door to the reality of how my world in the Hound facility was like. Maybe it had to do with the fact that he was unlike the other attendants which were always tied to themselves making socializing hard.

"No, it's fine!" I blurted, too emphatically. "I like the company. You can... stop by anytime."

The grin he tossed back literally melted me.

When he closed the door behind him, I dragged my body into the comfort of my bed. Rolling over onto my back, I draped an arm over my face, shoving my long hair out of the way.

"Seriously, Laura. What is wrong with you?" I muttered.

My only consolation was that if he was at the facility, he would most definitely be back.

Not because of my poor invitation, but because he had to do his job.

Whatever. I'd take it. And next time he came, I wouldn't be such a goofy mess. I'd spent enough hours in this room reading and re-reading the books Sarah brought me that I should be able to hold up my own intelligent conversation.

Just so long as he doesn't let out a smile.

Laying on my bed I read for a while, getting lost between the pages, cause my mind kept wandering back to a smiles that lit Damon face that afternoon. Finally, I gave myself a break, glancing over at the clock on the wall. 7:45. In fifteen minutes, the facility would begin shutting down for the night. There was no official curfew here, but considering all the doors locked at 8 p.m., the end result was pretty much the same.

But if I could beat time, I could still make it to the cafeteria and swipe a snack or more for later.

Sliding out of bed, I set the book on the nightstand pulling a pair of simple black flats from the closet. I no longer had to wear the facility gowns all the time like I had the first few years I was here, but my wardrobe choices never moved far beyond yoga pants and t-shirts.

When I stepped out of my room, the hallway was empty. I wasn't surprised. This place was dead quiet at night. I didn't consider myself a particularly adventurous person, but compared to some of the other patients who lived here, I was a wild child. We were each allowed to decorate our rooms with small alterations, but I was the only person who had any form posters or art on my walls that caught my fancy.

Those little things and my books were my ode to the outside world, a reminder that outside the walls of the facility a much better life resided.

The Hound treatment facility was a windowless structure, built underground to make it easier for them to protect us from airborne antibodies. There were levels below us that housed operating rooms, hospital beds, and medical equipment, but I lived my day to day life on the main floor, everything I needed was on that level and there was no reason to venture the other levels.

As I walked down the brightly lit, hallway. A wave of dizziness hit me out of nowhere. I staggered to a halt, sweat breaking out on my skin. Sharp pain tore through me, my muscles contracted, and I stumbled, falling to my knees.

Chapter 2-The Experience

The warm yellow lights along the hallway wall bounced in my vision as it began to turn blur.

I could feel the fire burning from within, my body shutting down. Pains lanced through my body gone one second and back with agonizing ferocity the next.

This shouldn't be happening, I was sure I had taken my medications

The fuzzy thoughts flowed through my brain, trying to find a place to land. The last time this ever happened was when I first arrived at the Hound facility and this was worse than anything I remembered. It felt different. More terrifying.

An alarm sounded, and footsteps raced down the hall.

"Laura?" a male voice called in the distance, but muffled whispers were all my ears could pick.

Professor! Professor!!

"She's burning" My insides ached as it felt like it was about to rupt out.

"When did this happen?" Professor Greyson demanded. "What went wrong?"

"I don't know, sir. She was fine, then she just went down."

"Christ. Hold her still."

Bright light assaulted my senses as strong hands latched onto my arms and legs with muffled groans that escaped my mouth.

"We need to get her downstairs." The light shining in my eyes cut off, and Professor Greyson's face swam in front of me. His brown eyes were anxious, and his eyebrows pinched together. "Put her on the gurney. Now!"

The hands holding my limbs carried me and placed me on a new higher surface. My body kept thrashing and jerking, and my brain felt like it was jingling in my skull. I tried to speak but I could barely form words.

Tight leather straps held firm across my chest, midsection, and legs, restraining the movement of my jerking body. Then the wheels of the gurney started to roll, and I was carried quickly down the hall, surrounded by doctors on both sides. Tears burst from my eyes, cascading down the sides of my face, as I stared up at the ceiling tiles that glided by over my head. The sight was so dreadfully familiar it sent dread wreathing through me.

There was a soft *ding*, and few moments later, I was wheeled into a large spaced elevator. Tense silence clouded the atmosphere, broken only by the fizzling sound of my body jerking and the rough grunts that escaped my tongue.

"Is it occurring?"

The soft voice was male, but I couldn't place who it belonged to. Maybe Alarick, one of the older male nurses on staff.

"Silence." Another voice shushed her.

Professor Greyson's face floated over me again, his hands now rested on my shoulders. "Laura. Do you hear me? You're going to be fine. We've got you. We're all here for you."

Even as the words escaped his mouth, I could feel myself fading. I held on to consciousness like a life raft, scared if I let myself slide under, I'd never return back. I'd seen other patients collapse and wheeled away, and they almost never came back.

No. I'm not ready to lose my life.

I fought against the muscle shudders rocking my body and tightened my hands into clenched fists, begging the goddess of luck to come through for me one more time. To let me be the medical miracle who fought against the odds. To give me one more chance to feel alive.

The elevator slid to a stop, and I was hurried down another long hallway, this one all white. I knew that because I'd been down here a few times before, although right now everything around me looked grey as my vision began narrowing to a pinprick.

"Shit! We're losing her! Hurry!"

Professor Greyson's panicked voice echoed through the hallway bouncing off the walls.

My eyes rolled back into my head, as blackness was finally overtaking me.

I drifted, lost in a web of darkness where my body didn't ache. There was nothing bad down there, but there was nothing good there either. It was just... nothing.

Flashes of light and sound momentarily burst into my consciousness as if someone had turned on a television with the volume going all the way up.

"Intubating now!"

A tube was forced down my throat, making me cough and gag.

Then darkness again.

Now I clung to the darkness, the quiet emptiness, not wanting to return to that room full of confusion and pain.

But I was pulled back by a sharp piercing sound. My eyes flew wide open as my body sprang upright, and I saw the leather straps that had held me down swinging in pieces beside me. My head whipped around, an untamed scream bolting from my mouth.

"Laura! Don't!" Professor Greyson's harsh cry pulled my attention, and I turned toward him. He plunged toward me, a needle in his hand. Before I could resist, the needle pierced through my skin, and with a pneumatic hiss, the contents emptied inside me.

I fell back, and the world went blank around me.

* * *

"Christ, that was close."

"I know. We should've been keeping an eye on her more carefully."

"With all due respect, Professor Greyson, I don't see how we could've watched her more closely. We got to her as quick as we could."

"And it almost wasn't as quick enough. I want her to be checked twice as often from now on. We're entering a very critical time."

Professor Greyson's voice was quiet and fatigue smelt round every sentence he spoke. Distress weighed down his words. As hazy memories of my attack began to filter into my mind, I felt overjoyed that he cared more about me. Professor Greyson was in charge of my treatment and though I was partly a lab project, I'd always felt like he personally invested in my well-being beyond that.

I was more than just a lab project to him. I was a person.

My eyelids flicked, and a small noise escaped me. The quiet discussion around me stopped, and when I opened my eyes, Professor Greyson stood there over me once again.

"Hey Laura." He smiled gently. "You gave us all quite a scare."

"I'm sorry." My mouth was bone dry.

"Hey, now. You don't have anything to be sorry for. It wasn't your fault at all. I'm just happy you're still with us."

"Me too."

"I'm going to get you something for the pain, okay? It'll weaken you a bit and give you a chance to rest more. We've got your temperature back to where they should be, but your body still needs some time to recuperate."

Deciding to lay quiet, I gave a small nod.

Professor Greyson hooked up a new bag to the IV drip, and seconds later, the cocktail of drugs took me away.

* * *

When I woke again, it was to a quiet room filled only with the beep of a heart rate monitor.

I blinked slowly. My body felt tired. I was propped up in a hospital bed, dressed in a medical gown.

But I couldn't feel the pain anymore.

A moment later, Sarah poked her head into the room.

"Alas! See who's awake!" The elderly nurse beamed at me as if I'd done something much more amusing than simply opening my eyes.

"Need something, dear?"

"Water," I said, my voice weakened though my throat didn't see to cause me pain anymore.

"Sure, one will do you better. Here." She took a plastic cup with a closed lid and straw off the counter. It contained a clear greenish liquid. "This will help with your electrolyte balance too. Drink up. I'll go get Professor Greyson."

Handing me the cup she turned away.

"Sarah?" I called. She stopped, looking back at me. "What happened? Why did I collapse?"

She sighed. "You had a little attack, dear. You really have been doing amazingly well, and you shouldn't let this bring you down. Professor Greyson adjusted your meds, and it seemed to be taking its effect that's all."

I nodded, although I knew it couldn't be simple as she made it sound. I'd almost lost my life.

"Okay. Thanks." She turned to leave, but my voice drew her attention again. "Hey, Sarah? My memory is kind of all fuzzy, but when we were in the elevator, I think you asked if 'it' was occurring. What did you mean? What was occurring?"

For a second, her face went blank. She stared at me, shook her head and gave out a sheepish laugh.

"It was nothing, sweetie. I didn't mean anything. I was just concerned about you. I wouldn't have said a word if I had known you could hear me; the last thing I want to do is frighten you." She walked over to the bed, cupping my cheek in her soft hand. "We've all gotten quite glued to you."

"Thanks, Sarah."

"Of course, dear." She stepped back. "I really don't want you to worry. I know that was scary, but it was just a minor attack. Professor Greyson says everything is back to normal now. I'll go get him so you can speak with him yourself."

She left through the door, leaving me alone in the room. I cleared my throat, as I brought the straw to my lips. The liquid was sweet and tasted like strawberries.

I was so grateful for everything Professor Greyson and his staff had done for me. And I was kind of attached to *them* too. They'd become like family to me, people I saw even more often than my own father. But doubt settled within as I recalled the look on Sarah's face.

She'd seemed almost... scared.

Before my thoughts could spiral any further, Professor Greyson walked in. The smile on his face was soothing. Glancing through my chart before meeting my gaze.

"Good news." He beamed down at me. "Everything is back to normal. You'll be able to return to your room now."

Chapter 3-Human Again

Professor Greyson had insisted on having them bring me to the main level in a wheelchair, which was disheartening. But he had my life in his hands, and my survival depended on following his orders exactly.

That, and a little drop of luck.

I was a mess when I finally got to my room. I'd been down in the lab for over a week so they could keep an eye on me as I recovered from my attack. But now I felt disgusting from several days without a bath.

Mariana, a nurse with a loud laugh, wheeled me inside.

Damon looked up in surprise from where he was changing the sheets on my bed. "Oh, hey!" He peered at me more closely. "Looking good?"

My cheeks lit up, and I looked down, allowing my tangled brown hair cover my face. "Yeah, I'm fine. I just need a shower."

I stood up, anxious to wash off the smell that was hovered round my body as I was to get out of Damon's sight. But Professor Greyson obviously had a good reason for ordering the wheelchair—my legs gave way as soon as I put all my weight on them, and I tripped.

Damon darted toward me, his grey-blue eyes flashing with concern, and caught me under the arms before I went down. The muscles of his large biceps contracted against his sleeves, although it didn't look like he was taking any effort to hold me up.

I blinked up at him, lost in the soft blue of his eyes. My arms had gone around his neck instinctively, and his skin was warm under my fingertips.

He was taller than I'd realized. He glanced over my shoulder at Mariana and set me back gently in the wheelchair.

He cleared his throat. "Well, I'll leave you to it. Mariana, can you finish the bed?"

"Sure."

Keeping his head down, Damon slipped past us and out the door. A trickle of embarrassment travelled down my spine. Damn it. He'd seemed really anxious to get out of here. Maybe I did stink.

Mariana helped me to the seat in the shower then left the door cracked while she returned to make up the bed.

When I finally felt clean, I used a rail on the side of the shower to help pull me to my feet. My legs held firm to the ground this time, although I felt a little wobbly. Professor Greyson seemed to know I was okay, so this was just in all probability regular muscle weakness from being bed ridden for a week. I walked slowly out of the shower halfway dressed by the time Mariana strode back in.

"Look at you!" She clapped her hands. "Back on your feet already. You'll be back to the customary in no time! Professor Greyson has you booked for training sessions every day of this week from tomorrow. He doesn't want you to lose too much because of the attack."

I groaned. "*Tomorrow?*"

Mariana helped me out of the bathroom and to my bed, although I rarely needed her steadying hand anymore. My legs were recovering fast. She left few minutes later, reminding me to use the call button if I wanted anything.

I spent the rest of the day in my room, reading and recovering. I'd become an expert in passing time over the years, but now I found myself oddly restless — so much so that by the following day, I was actually looking forward to my training sessions.

"Glad to see you back on your feet."

Ernie smiled at me as I approached. She was short and broad, all stocky muscle and spiky dark hair. I was in pretty good shape, thanks to her.

"Good to be back on my feet." I smiled, pushing away the memory of me stumbling of my wheelchair. Nothing frightened me as much as feeling weak.

Ernie noticed the strained expression on my face and clapped me heavily by the arm. "Don't worry. We'll get you back in shape in no time. You're one of my best patients. I won't give you up."

I nodded, gathering up my long brown hair into a tight ponytail. Over the next hour, she put me through couple of drills, mostly bodyweight exercises that tested my strength and agility. I *had* lost some ground after the week in the lab, but as my heart rate geared up, I could feel my body falling into shape again.

By the end of the week, I could almost forget my brush with death had ever happened.

Until my father paid a visit.

* * *

"Dad, I'm okay!"

It had been my dad and I since I was little, my mum had died after gracing me the privilege to breath earth's air.

But my dad didn't believe me, because I could feel his grip on me getting tightened further.

"I was very worried about you, baby girl."

I sighed, wrapping my arms around him. Sometimes I feel like he had forgotten I'd been growing up this whole time.

Sometimes I felt that way too. I was twenty-five, but I had no clue how to live the age.

"Are you all right? Professor Greyson said your CBC looks good, but tell me how do you *feel*?"

Looking away I avoided his gaze. "I feel… fine."

I walked over to the small couch set against the back wall and plunk onto it. My dad followed, watching me carefully. Leaning against one end, I turned to look at him.

"I do feel fine, Dad. That's the problem. I went from fine, to almost dead in the space of one week. It makes me..." I held back, fighting the tears that were about to run down my face. "It makes me think this will never ever be over."

With understanding in his every expression he patted me on the hand, his gaze fixed on my sad face.

"It will be, Laura. One day, you'll be freed. Professor Greyson and his staff are working so hard. You've come so far. You just have to keep believing."

Could I live my whole life like this? Confined to this facility—never stepping foot outside its walls? Never experiencing something as basic as going on a date?

Was that really a life worth living?

And even more terrifying, what would happen if the facility felt the same way? If my illness was incurable? Would they kick me out of here eventually?

My dad seemed to read all the doubts crossing my mind as if I'd spoken them out loud. "Don't give up, Laura. I know it's hard. But nothing has changed. You're still the fighter you always were. Just keep doing what Professor Greyson tells you, and bet it you'll beat this."

I leaned into him touch, closing my eyes. I wouldn't want him to see the doubt that still resided in them.

When I met him gaze again, I forced a smile. "Thanks, Dad. But enough about me. How are you?"

He smiled. "I'm good."

I giggled. "What are you planning for the summer?"

He relaxed back into the couch cushions, pondering. "Read some books. And visit you a lot more."

"That would be great."

I worried about him. With my mum gone and his only child stuck in a facility a couple of hours from his home in Houston, I hoped he wasn't lonely. Then he sat up straighter, plucking his bag that laid on the couch beside him. "Oh, I almost forgot. I brought you something!"

He pulled several books out of his bag, and my face brightened with genuine excitement for the first time since he'd arrived. He always knew how to get me from my down times.

We spent several more hours talking and laughing, and by the time he left, I felt quite better.

But as the door closed behind him, a dark cloud rolled into the room. I stared in space, and despite the years I'd lived here, it felt sterile.

How much longer would I live here like this?

But what other choice did I have?

Chapter 4 -Attack on Hound

"How have you been fairing, Laura?" I clinched my jaw. The number of times I'd been asked that over the course of my life was staggering. I knew the question meant good, but I'd have given anything to never hear those words...... again.

"Fine."

"That's great," Professor Greyson said approvingly. His face hovered from mine as he shone a small light into my eyes. And my gaze darted around the room like a butterfly, flitting from place to place without really landing on anything.

"Look up," he directed. I obeyed. "Good. And down."

I followed his directive, and he nodded with satisfaction before moving around to peer into each ear.

"How are your new meds treating you?"

"Fine." I tensed as his hands adjusted the back of my facility gown to place the end of his stethoscope in between my shoulder blades. His fingers cold. "I've been a little apathetic, especially at night, but not too bad."

"That's fine." His voice calm and soothing. "That's an expected side effect. If it gets to be too much, we can adjust your dose. Breathe in."

My ribs expanded as I pulled in a lungful of air. Then I released it slowly. The facility gown was tied at the back of my neck, but all I had on beneath it was a pair of underwear, and as Professor Greyson's cold fingers moved the stethoscope to a new spot on my back, goose bumps rose on my arms.

He listened to me take a few more deep breaths before pulling the stethoscope out of his ears and folding it around his neck. He retied the gown at my back, then grabbed my chart and sat on his stool.

"Well, everything looks good, Laura. I think we're back on track. Have any questions for me?"

"Do you think I'm going to die in here?"

Professor Greyson stopped writing on my chart.

He looked up at me. "Why do you say that, Laura?"

I swallowed, wishing I could take back what I'd just. I had no idea why I'd suddenly lost my faith in the healing process. I wanted to get my equilibrium back, but I had no idea where to find it.

"I… I don't know. I guess lately I've just started to wonder if I'll ever be cured. I mean, what if I'm not? Will you guys take care of me forever?"

Professor Greyson regarded me seriously, resting his elbows on his knees and lacing his fingers together. "I can't say anything with one hundred percent certainty, you know that. But I will tell you this, Laura. Everyone in this facility is invested in you. You are important to us. Beyond the science. Beyond the medicine. *You* are mean a lot to us."

"Thanks, Professor Greyson." I scratched my ear, blushing slightly. "I guess it's good to know you guys see me as more than my disease."

"You're much more than that, Laura." He smiled, rubbing the inside of his wrist with the thumb of his opposite hand. "There are things in this world even science can't explain yet. Faith is important. "I'm not going to tell you who to pray to, but I will tell you it's important that you believe in something.

"How do you find the balance?" I asked. "Between faith and science?"

Professor Greyson's smile widened, and his eyes beamed with excitement. "I don't need to, Laura. At some point, the two meet. And that's where miracles happen."

His enthusiasm was contagious, and I found a little of my old confidence returning.

That's where miracles happen.

I could beat the odds.

Running a hand down my arm I grinned back at him. "I like that. Thanks, Professor Greyson."

"No worries, Laura." He moved back towards the desk at the corner, taking a look at my chart. "Now, I've got you—"

A sound in the distance interrupted him, and he broke off abruptly.

The sound came again.

A rapid *pop-pop-pop,* echoed down the hall.

"What's that?"

Even as I asked, a cold feeling rushed through me, and my heart grew cold in my chest.

Before he could answer, shouts echoed from down the hallway, followed by the sound of feet pounding against the floor. An alarm blared through the facility, so loud. I'd never heard a siren like this, not even when one of the patients ha an attack like I had.

Professor Greyson's froze. His eyes went wide, and shocked expression registered on his face.

I threw my hands over my ears, trying to block out the screeching siren as I yelled over its noise. "What's happening?"

He didn't answer.

My heart was galloping in my rib cage now, confusion ruling my insides. Whatever this was, it wasn't normal.

The handle of the only door into the room rattled. I yelped, turning toward it. The door didn't open, and the handle shook harder. *Locked.* Had it always been locked? Or was it some kind of automatic shutdown that came along with the sirens?

It mattered not in a second though, because two more loud pops sounded, and the lock blew away. The door flew open as someone kicked it from the other side, and Professor Greyson finally leapt into action. He threw himself toward me. His hand latched around my upper arm, dragging me off the exam table.

Another pop of gunfire filled the room, louder and closer this time, and I screamed. Professor Greyson grunted in pain, as he released his grip on me.

Staggering backward, going down near a medical supply cabinet along the wall.

I stood in the middle of the room numb, as the man with the gun strode inside, his steps smooth and controlled as a stalking cat. He was striking, with short, brown hair and a crooked nose that looked like it'd been broken.

He moved the gun around the room before turning it to Professor Greyson again.

"Where's Luke?" he growled.

"Luke?" Professor Greyson inched backward toward the wall. "I... I don't know who that is."

"Damnit." The man sneered in disgust. "Of course you don't.

More shouts echoed from outside. Raised, angry voices. More feet running. I stood paralyzed, my gaze darting between the intruder and Professor Greyson.

"I don't know a thing you're saying," Professor Greyson gasped. He'd wedged himself into a nook between the cabinet and the wall.

"Luke!" the man repeated, both hands steadying his weapon. He was at the compound outside San Diego before they shut it down. Is he here?"

The fear that had twisted Professor Greyson's faded, replaced by an almost condescending glare. "No. He's not here."

The new man swore under his breath. His gaze flicked to me, and for the first time since he'd entered, he seemed to truly take me in. His attention lingered on me for a second too long... and in that second, Professor Greyson moved.

He slid his left hand behind the medical supply cabinet. When he pulled it out, a gun was clutched in his grip.

The intruder's head whipped back toward him, his hand tightening on his own weapon.

Two shots broke into the air.

Chapter 5 –The Escape

I closed my ears as the gunshots rang out, into the void of chaos.

A hole appeared in the wall inches from Professor's head, and the shot he'd fired toward the intruder had gone wide.

The man dove to the side as Professor Greyson aimed again. A third shot echoed in the room as the man slammed into me, bringing me to the floor with a heavy thud. We landed behind the large metal table, separating us from Professor Greyson.

The man rolled off me, ejecting the magazine from his handgun. He reached into his back pocket then jammed another magazine into his weapon. Another shot hit the metal table, sending up a loud metallic ringing noise.

I pulled my arms and legs in tight. I had no idea what was happening, why Professor Greyson had a gun, or who the intruder was, but my body instinctively made itself smaller, avoiding a stray bullet.

Whipping his arm over the top of the metal table, the intruder let off another shot. A small medical supply tray toppled as Professor Greyson threw himself away from the wall.

As the metal tray hit the floor with a clang, scattering needles, and antiseptic, the intruder grabbed my hand, pulling me to my feet. He pulled me toward the door, laying down suppressing gunfire over my shoulder.

"Come on! I'll get you out of here!" he yelled. I saw his lips move, but his words sounded muffled and hazy.

Before I could even sort through what he wanted, we were running through the hall. The man had a tight grip on my hand that I could barely feel my fingers, and I was in a state of shock that all I could do was to keep running. The siren continued to blare. The man shot the lock off a staff door and pulled me through, dragging me up a set of stairs.

"Up here. Go!"

My uncoordinated feet slipped halfway, and I smashed my shin into the concrete stair, sending pain into my leg. I fell down three steps and almost tumbled all the way back to the landing, but the intruder still had a firm grip on me.

He hauled me up, holding the gun in his other hand. My bare feet scrabbled at the concrete until I found my footing, and then we were running again.

On the next floor, he shoved open the door with his shoulder, pointing his gun into the hallway as he whipped his head back and forth.

This was a floor I'd never been on before. I hadn't even known it existed. The hallway up here was clean and sterile. But the calming effect was destroyed by the alarm that seemed to blare even more loudly up here.

The man pulled me out of the stairwell and down the hall. His heavy boots rang loudly on the polished marble while my bare feet beat a discordant rhythm. His grip on my hand finally loosened a bit, allowing me to wiggle my fingers. We passed an intersecting hallway, and I glanced down it as we hurried by.

My breath stuck in my throat.

Dad.

I'd only caught a fast glimpse down the hall, but I was definitely sure I'd seen him. My dad was here.

Without even thinking, I pulled my hand from the man's grasp. The action took him by surprise, which probably was the reason I managed to break his grip.

He called out behind me, but I didn't hear him. I didn't even worry about the fact that he might shoot me in the back as I ran away.

All I knew was that dad was here, and I had to get to him.

I careened around the corner into the new hallway, running. My dad stood at the end of the hall where it met another hallway, and he looked up at the sight of me. His eyes went wide. My heart clinched with relief and worry.

I needed to tell him to get out of here.

Putting on an extra burst of speed, I ran toward him.

He blinked twice then reached behind him, pulling something from the waistband of his jeans.

When his hands reappeared, time seemed to slow.

A gun.

My dad was holding a gun, its thick black grip resting easily in the palm of his hand. His other hand came up to meet it, cradling the butt of the gun as he steadied it, bringing it up to aim straight at me.

My feet skidded on the slippery marble floor as my body tried to reverse its forward trajectory very fast, and I went down hard on my ass. A shot pierced the air, and my I froze. A bullet whizzed over my head, exactly where my torso had been just seconds earlier.

Shock took over me.

I couldn't move.

I couldn't breathe.

Dad. What are you doing?

He began to walk toward me, bringing down his arms a bit to aim the barrel toward my head.

I stared at it. Saw the clean, dark lines of the metal, the small hole at the end where a bullet would burst forth to end my life. Saw the gentle but firm way he held it in his grip. His arms were braced, locked out in front of him, and his lips were set in a thin, firm line.

His eyes were unreadable.

Fear lanced through me, but it couldn't break through the haze of confusion. I scrabbled backward on my butt. But I wasn't moving fast enough. There was nowhere to go. My dad took another step forward, adjusting his grip on the gun slightly —

A figure burst into the hallway from the intersecting corridor behind him.

Before he could turn toward him, he tackled him, bringing him down with a loud yell. As he and my dad wrestled for control of the gun in his hand.

"Dad!"

Heart beating, I made a move toward them — to help him? Or to help the new stranger? — but before I could act, the man tore the gun from my dad's grip. In one swift movement, he brought the butt of it down against the side of his head.

I heard the crack. *Felt* it down my soul.

My dad's head whipped to the side, then he went still.

Blood leaking from the wound at his temple.

"Fuck." The large man, still across him, checked his gun for bullets then shoved the magazine back into the weapon. He looked up, taking me in at a glance before shifting his gaze over my shoulder. "This turned into a fucking shit show."

"Yeah. We need to get out of here. Now."

The voice came from behind me, and when I turned to look, the man with the slightly bent nose and brown hair was striding quickly down the hall toward us, his gun still held at the ready.

"Agreed."

The men continued to confer, each keeping their gun aimed down one end of the corridor in watchful suspense.

But I stopped listening.

I couldn't stop staring at the prone figure of my father. I had ended up pressed against the wall, and I wanted to crawl toward him, wanted to make sure he was okay — but I couldn't get my body to move.

When I turned the corner and ran toward him, there had been no one else in the hallway with us. It'd been just me and my dad... and he'd shot at me.

He'd aimed right for my heart and fired.

I couldn't process that fact, no matter how many times my terrified mind shouted the words. His face was still, and except for the blood oozing from his temple, he looked exactly like he did when he came to visit me and fell asleep on my couch after one of our long discussions.

Finally, my body did move. Slowly, I crawled toward him.

My eyes were locked on my dad's chest, trying to pick up the rise and fall that would tell me if he was still breathing. I reached out for him slowly, but movement at the end of the hall froze me.

My body tensed, and I braced for more gunfire.

But none came.

"Marcus! Anything?" the man who'd tackled my dad called out.

"What does it fucking look like?"

Two new men jogged down the hall toward us. The one who'd spoken had curly black hair and a dark scowl on his face. The other was...

"Damon?"

The word stuck in my throat, half whisper and half croak, as my brain overloaded completely.

Damon looked down at me. He wasn't smiling now, but even with the serious expression on his face, there was something about him that radiated warmth and kindness. He did a double-take when he saw me, his eyes widening.

The man who had burst into the exam room at the beginning of this nightmare shook his head at the black-haired newcomer. "Luke's not here, Marcus. I'm sorry."

"You don't know that!" Marcus argued. "He could be hidden somewhere! This place is a totally different setup than the San Diego complex. Maybe they've got her in a separate wing! Maybe—"

Damon broke his gaze away from me and looked up at his friend. "Jack's right. I've been here for a month, and I haven't found anything like that. This place is run by a small staff, but they've definitely called for backup by now. If we don't get out soon, we're never ever getting out."

"But if she's here—!"

"Dude!" The mocha-skinned man grabbed a fistful of Marcus's shirt, getting into his face. "Let it go! He wouldn't want you to give up your life trying to get him out. And if you die here, you'll never find him. We'll try again. But right now, *we have to go.*"

Marcus's lips curled up in a snarl. The two men were almost nose to nose, their foreheads practically touching. For a moment, thick tension hung in the air between them, and I almost expected Marcus to swing his gun around and shoot the other man in the head. He looked mad enough to try it.

Then he blinked. His jaw ticked and his nostrils flared, but he nodded stiffly. "We *will* try again, Jonathan."

It sounded almost like a threat. But the man staring him down—Jonathan—didn't seem to take it that way. He released his grip on Marcus's shirt and slapped him on the chest. "Always, brother."

I stared dumbly up at them all. I felt like I was watching an action movie, a spectator removed from everything around me. My body had gone numb, and the continuous shrill whine of the alarm felt like it had permeated my brain, like it would never stop.

"Come on, Laura. We'll get you out of here."

Damon held his hand down to me. I blinked at it, my toes curling into the cold marble beneath my feet. I didn't want to go anywhere. I couldn't leave this place. I was sick—I needed here to survive.

This all had to be some huge misunderstanding, some intensely vivid nightmare.

"We got to go!" Jack called, shifting his gaze down the opposite end of the hallway and raising his gun.

The sound of pounding feet rumbled like thunder under the high pitch of the alarm, and a moment later, half a dozen guards dressed in tactical gear rounded the corner.

Fear iced my blood.

Whatever backup these three men had been worried about, had arrived.

Chapter 6-The New World

Gunshots echoed in the confined space of the corridor, and a hand—I wasn't even sure whose—reached down, hauling me to my feet. I found myself surrounded by three large bodies, racing down the hall of this unfamiliar level of the Hound Facility.

More shots sounded, even as we outraced the men behind us. One of the guys bringing up the rear of our group grunted, his footsteps faltering briefly.

"Jonathan? Are you hit?" Damon called.

"Yup."

"You all right?"

"Yup."

The word was curt, as if running down a hallway getting shot at was something, he did so often it wasn't worth remarking upon.

Who the hell were these men?

And what did they want with me?

My body was jostled between the large men as we careened around a corner. The one called Marcus kicked open a door and led us up another set of access stair. This time I managed to keep my feet under me, but just barely. Damon switched his grip on me to my elbow, steadying me.

We raced up three flights of stairs, ducking every time one of the men chasing us shot up through the stairwell. My breath came in sharp gasps by the time

Marcus shoved open the door at the top landing, and Damon pulled me through.

Light nearly blindfolded me.

I staggered, blinking in the sudden onslaught of sunlight. The air was warm and slightly humid, and the asphalt beneath my bare feet was hot.

Before I could fully absorb the fact that I was outside, we were moving again, running across a small parking lot toward a row of parked cars. I threw a look back over my shoulder. The building we'd emerged from was small and innocuous-looking. It was a single story structure made of plain brown brick. Nothing about it gave any hint of the levels it housed underground, beneath the surface.

As I watched, the door we'd exited through opened again.

The first man to emerge was huge, tall as a tree and muscled like a TV wrestler. His neck was as wide as his head, and his blond hair was cropped short. There was a hard look on his face, and when my gaze met his, my blood ran cold. I thought I knew everyone at the Hound Facility, but I'd never seen this guy before.

If I had, I was sure he would've haunted my nightmares.

He strode toward us, raising his gun.

Before he could fire, I was yanked sharply to the side, bringing my attention back to my immediate surroundings. Damon dragged me behind a large SUV, blocking us from the approaching guards. Jack smashed out the driver's side window and unlocked the doors while Marcus shot around the front of the car, slowing our pursuers.

Yanking open the back door, Damon picked me up and practically threw me inside. I landed on the soft leather seat and scrambled to sit up.

"Now would be a great time to show off those hot-wiring skills you always brag about!" Damon called to Jack, sliding in beside me and pushing my head down with a hand at the back of my neck.

"I'm already on it." Jack's voice was tense with concentration.

A moment later, the engine roared to life.

"Tires!" he yelled to the Marcus still outside the car.

I had no idea what that meant, but when I lifted my head a little, I saw the guy called Marcus turn his gun toward the other cars in the parking lot. While Damon continued to shoot at the guards, who'd taken cover around the side of the building, Marcus systematically shot out the tires of all the vehicles around us.

Smart.

My numb brain was reduced to processing a single thought at a time. I couldn't comprehend the entirety of what was happening to me, the nuclear bomb that had just gone off in my simple life. But I could see that these men worked well together. That they were smart.

Jack gunned the engine as Marcus piled inside. Then we peeled out.

I snuck a peek behind us as we sped toward the parking lot's exit. The men in black tactical gear raced out from where they'd taken cover. Several of them looked at the cars with punctured tires, and a few shot after us. But the big blond man, who towered almost a foot above his compatriots, didn't waste time with either of those things. He turned and jogged purposefully around the far side of the building.

Were there other cars over there? What had he and his men arrived in?

Bullets ricocheted off the back of the SUV, and Damon put his hand on the back of my head again. I stared at my bare feet as the men's shouts filled the car and a sudden left turn shoved Damon's large, hard body against mine.

"Damn it! That fucking blond is behind us!" someone called.

"Hold on." Jack's voice was stern, and the car turned wildly again, sending me sliding the other way. I clinched my eyes shut and gritted my teeth. Another shot resounded from the back of the car, making my heart leap into my throat.

This isn't real. None of this is.

Maybe the new meds Professor Greyson had given me were messing with my system, causing hallucinations. Maybe I was inside the facility right now being rushed into the lab. But then why were the smells of metal, gunpowder so strong in my nostrils? Why was the back seat of the SUV full of Diet Coke cans?

Would I really dream that up?

"You all right, Jonathan? Where'd they get you?" Damon asked, his voice taut with concern.

"Bullet grazed my arm. I'm fine."

I lost track of the twists and turns the car took as we sped down the road, Jonathan calling out directions to Jack. When I finally peeked out the window, I saw that we were in a rural area, with trees lining the sides of the road. Jack made fewer sharp turns, but he never let up on the accelerator as the inside of the car settled into a tense silence.

Finally, the car shuddered slightly, slowing.

"Shit. SUV driver didn't fill up their tank. We're almost out of gas," Jack muttered. "We're about eight miles from our stash."

"Just as well. If we drove any closer, we'd risk leading them right to us." Damon spoke beside me, his voice soft. He'd let up his hold on my head, but I remained bent over, curled into myself, as if by making myself as small as possible, I could escape my new reality. "It's better if we cover the last bit on foot."

The car lurched again, slowing even more.

"Not like we have any fucking choice." Jack chuckled.

With a final shudder, the car eased to a stop. The front doors opened, and I heard the passenger side door open too. A moment later, strong hands slid around my waist. Damon tugged me gently out of the car after him. The gravel on the roadside bit into my feet, and when I stumbled, he swept me up into his arms.

I shut my eyes, burying my face in his warm blue fabric. He was the only one of the three guys who wasn't dressed in black, loaded down with weapons, and somehow that made him slightly less terrifying. In my head, I could still pretend he was just "Damon the cute attendant," not some kind of renegade soldier who'd kidnapped me in a blaze of gunfire.

"You just going to carry her the whole way?" Jonathan sounded slightly amused and annoyed.

"Yeah, man. I am," Damon shot back. "You think she's going to walk like this?"

"As long as it doesn't slow us down. If she slows us down, we do away with her."

That was Marcus, and the hard edge to his voice made my blood run cold. He wasn't joking.

Damon didn't answer, but his grip on me tightened a little, so much that I felt tears sting my eyes. At least one of these men didn't want me to die—not that any of them would truly be able to stop it. I'd been taken from the Hound medical complex, the one place where I was safe.

Outside, exposed to a number of unknown pathogens, how long would I last? How long before my body turned on itself again?

And this time, there would be no doctors to rush me into emergency care, no one to adjust my meds and monitor my vitals. Just four broad-shouldered men who, no matter how well trained they were with weaponries, possible didn't know a thing about medicine.

I'm going to perish out here.

That thought frightened me, but not as much as it should have. I didn't want to die—had spent all those years in the Hound Facility fighting against death. But right now, in my shocked, hollowed out state, struggling to push away the memory of my Father pointing a gun at my head, a small part of me welcomed the idea of oblivion. Of peace.

The men had started to move. My head shoved against Damon's shoulder as he ran, moving speedily through the woods with long, even strides, as if he carried no burden at all.

After a while, a loud whoosh sound reached my ears. Water?

Damon's voice rumbled in his chest as he mumbled, "Sorry, Laura. We gotta go in."

Before I could even make up the words to ask what he intended, ice-cold water touched my butt, soaking through my underwear and facility gown instantly. I gasped and jolted in his arms, and he looked down at me apologetically as he strode deeper into the river.

"We need to move downstream a bit. With a bit of luck, it'll make our trail harder to pick up."

I had only a vague idea what he meant by that, but I didn't complain. Marcus shot me a glare out of the corner of his eye as he plodded through the water ahead of us, and I pressed my face back against Damon's chest as the water rose higher up my body. My entire midsection was underwater, and occasionally my feet and toes dipped under too. Those parts slowly went numb, while angry goose bumps covered the rest of my skin, making my entire body ache.

We walked through the water for so long I lost track of time. By the time we emerged downstream, the light had changed around us. We were in a deeply wooded area, but the gloom wasn't just from the canopy overhead. The sun was setting.

And still, the men didn't stop.

They continued through the woods, exchanging quiet words from time to time. My soggy gown clung to my body — as we'd walked through the river, the water had slowly worked its way up, soaking through even the fabric that wasn't submerged.

"There. Up ahead."

"Thank fuck."

Damon's steps sped up, and I moved myself slowly, looking up in time to see a small shelter ahead of us. It looked very homemade, consisting of a brown tarp slung between several closely spaced trees. Leaves and twigs were scattered across the top of the tarp, some hanging over the sides. Several large packs rested at the bases of the trees.

We walked beneath the tarp, which dipped to some extent in the middle but was high enough to allow the men to stand upright. Damon lowered me gently to my feet, and I staggered away from him like a baby deer. It was hard to stand—I was cold and dog-tired and so emotionally strung out, I felt high. The world dipped and swayed in my vision, but I clenched my teeth, fighting to remain upright.

For a moment, the four of us just stood in silence. A bird called in the distance.

Then, suddenly, the black-haired man named Marcus screamed.

As if he'd held back his feelings for too long, he unleashed a untamed shriek, a torrent of angry curses spilling from his lips. Turning, he struck out at a nearby tree trunk, smashing his fists against it until his knuckles were raw and bloody.

I'd never seen someone so aggressively angry in all my life. Unconsciously, I shrivelled away from him, bumping into a muscled chest behind me. Strong arms with dark skin wrapped around me, but before I could disentangle myself from Jack's grip, Marcus rounded on me. His piercing blue eyes flashed with rage—and pain. Such a deep, soul-splintering pain that the sight almost called tears to my own eyes.

He hauled me from Jack's grip, his bloody fingers leaving red streaks on the damp fabric of my sleeves. He shook me roughly, his lips curling back in a snarl.

"Where is she? Sarah! Was she there? Did they kill her? Answer me!"

My brain rattled in my skull as he shook me again, and nausea churned my stomach.

"What the fuck did they do to him? What did *you* do?" His broad chest rose and fell quickly, and he gripped my arms so tight it hurt. *"Where is he?"*

"I—" My tongue felt thick, my lips numb. My teeth chattered uncontrollably. "I d-don't—know what you're—t-talking about. I didn't do—"

Damon stepped forward, his gray eyes flashing. He shoved his friend away from me. "She didn't do anything, Marcus! Come on. Does she look like a fucking lap dog to you? She's as blameless as any one of us."

Without missing a beat, Marcus rounded on him. "Oh yeah? Then why was—"

But the rest of his angry words were swallowed up by the dull shriek that filled my ears. My body shivered so hard it began to shake convulsively, and my knees buckled.

Oh no.

This was it.

My body had been strained to the breaking point, and my illness, having lain in wait for so long, would finally swoop in to finish me. *Please, God. Just let it be quick.*

Chapter 7-Meeting the Hybrids

Strong hands caught me before I crumpled to the ground. I watched Marcus stare at me with malicious, icy eyes as Damon and Jack lowered me gently to the ground.

"Jesus fuck! She's freezing." Damon bit his lip. "Damn it, Laura, why didn't you say anything?"

"I'm n-not c-cold. I'm s-sick."

"You *are* cold. And wet. Shit, your fingers are like ice."

Damon grimaced, wrapping his large hand around one of mine. My numb fingers could barely feel the pressure of his grip.

Marcus backed up a few paces, his expression a mixture of guilt, anger, and pain. Then he turned and raced off into the woods.

"Marcus!" Jack called, looking up from where he knelt at my feet.

My toes peeked out from between his hands, almost blue in the waning light. Shocks still wracked my body, making it hard to speak, hard to breathe.

"Let him go. He needs to shift; he'll feel better after he does." Jack stared after Marcus, grimacing.

"We need to get some dry clothes on her." Damon jerked his chin toward one of the packs set against a tree trunk. "Jack, grab that bag. The clothes we brought for Luke should fit her."

"Oh, man." Jack shook his head, a humourless giggle echoing from his lips as his hands rubbed my feet in a quick motion. "Marcus is going to fucking love this."

"Well, someone should use them, right?" Damon shot back. "And he's not here, is he?"

"Not arguing. Just sayin'."

I tried to follow their discussion, but all I could focus on were the strong, rough-skinned fingers bringing life back to my hands and feet. My muscles still contracted involuntarily, but as Damon and Jack massaged my chilled skin, some feeling began to return to my extremities.

Jack dropped the large backpack on the ground next to me and squatted down, rifling around inside it. "Here. Got pants and a shirt, and socks and shoes. I don't know shit about sizes, but they look like they'll fit."

Hovering above me, Damon met Jack's eyes. "Do you want to…?"

"Undress her? What do I look like, a fucking leech?"

"Jesus Christ. Move." Jack pushed Damon away from me, as he helped me sit up. He cupped the sides of my face, his large hands unexpectedly gentle. "Listen, we've got to get you into warm clothes, okay? We're going to take your gown off. There's nobody else in these woods, and none of us will look. We promise. Is that all right? Damon will stand guard."

I jerked my head up and down quickly. If my body was attacking itself from the inside, a fresh set of clothes wouldn't do much to save me from death. But I craved warmth on a primal level, and at this point, I didn't care who saw me naked in the process.

"Okay. Pants first."

Jack grabbed the pair of pants and helped me work my feet through each leg. When he bunched up around my thighs, he leveraged me to my feet—although without him holding me up, I wouldn't have stayed vertical. He slid the pants all the way up, reaching under my wet hospital gown to work them over my hips.

When he moved to pull the zipper up, a small breath escaped my lips.

I'd never been touched by any man as intimately as I'd been touched by these men today. It felt foreign and strange, but not altogether unpleasant. Despite the cloud of confusion and fear, and the illness devastating my system, I registered each touch as if they were mapping out uncharted places on my body.

When Jack slipped the top button closed, his gaze rose to meet mine. Heat sputtered in his dark eyes, and his voice was low when he spoke.

"Now the shirt."

I nodded, suddenly aware of how stiff my nipples were beneath the cold, wet gown. It clung to my body, the translucent fabric revealing so much I might as well be naked already. I had an urge to clamp my hands over my breasts, but instead, I remained perfectly still as Jack held me up with a firm grip on my hips and Damon untied the back of the gown.

Then they switched. Damon supported my weight while Jack slid the gown off my arms. I could tell he was trying to keep his promise, but for the briefest moment, his gaze flicked to my chest.

I swallowed, a confusing mixture of emotions whirling through me as my skin reacted to his look as though it were a physical touch.

The mocha-skinned man cleared his throat and averted his gaze, tugging the shirt down over my head before helping me slip my arms through and pulling it down the rest of the way.

He seemed to relax as soon as I was fully dressed, and it was only then that I realized how nervous he'd been before—as if he'd been holding himself in check somehow.

They lowered me down to sit on the ground, and I found myself cradled between Damon's legs, my back pressed to his front. His clothes were still damp from the river, but he radiated so much body heat, I scarcely cared.

"Uh, you guys look like you got this." Jack glanced over his shoulder from where he'd been keeping lookout. "I'm gonna go find Marcus. Make sure he doesn't do anything stupid."

"Good idea," Damon told him. "We don't need him shrieking all night. Keep him calm. And stay close."

"Yeah." Jack walked out from under the cover of the tarp. Then he paused and turned back, glancing down at me. "Hey, what's your name?"

I blinked, my brain so vague I almost forgot the answer for a second before I whispered, "A-Laura."

He nodded, regarding me thoughtfully. He looked like he smiled a lot, but he wasn't smiling now. "Laura. Welcome to the pack. I'm glad you're okay."

I didn't respond, and after a second he shot me a lopsided grin. He gave a quick salute to the other two men before disappearing into the woods.

Where was he going? Where had the angry one with curly black hair gone? I didn't understand what was going on, and I found myself unusually concerned about the strangers who had abducted me.

Why should I give a single shit what happens to any of them? Is this what Stockholm syndrome feels like?

Maybe it was, but at the moment, I wasn't sure I cared.

Damon grabbed my feet, working them over with his hands just like Jack had done, while he wrapped his arms over mine, completely enveloping my fists in his larger ones. Warmth finally began to sink back into my bones, and my body stopped quivering.

But as the cold slipped away, so did the last of my strength.

My eyelids drooped, and nothing I did could force them open again.

"I can't stay out here. I'm... sick..." I murmured, clinging to consciousness. They needed to know. They needed to understand. "I have to... go back. I don't want to die."

Damon made a sound low in his throat. The movement of his hands slowed, and he squeezed my feet in his warm grip.

He let out a deep breath. His words tickled my ear as he spoke in a quiet voice.

"You're not sick, Laura; you never were. We will not let you die." There was a beat before words graced his tongue again. "And you can't ever go back there."

Chapter 8 -Laura's New Home?

In my dream, I saw my Father's face. He sat on the couch in my small room at the Hound Facility, talking and laughing with me like we always did. His caramel brown eyes were warm and open.

Sweet.

Loving.

And then they changed.

The light behind her eyes went out, and those once-kind windows to his soul became as absolute and empty as black holes. And as the light inside them dimmed, the rest of his expression shifted too, the soft wrinkles on his face hardening to cold lines. One corner of his mouth lifted in a slight sneer as she reached behind him, pulling a gun from and aiming the barrel right between my eyes.

Cold steel pressed against my forehead. But I knew it would be scalding hot after the gun fired.

After the bullet pierced my brain.

The barrel would smoke, and blood would splatter, and my life would end in a single loud bang.

My dad tilted his head to the side, regarding me where I sat frozen in fear.

"I wasted too many years of my life pretending to love you, Laura."

His voice wasn't the same. Nothing was the same. The Man I loved, who'd comforted me when I was sick, who'd visited me every week without fail – who had uprooted his life to be near me while I underwent treatment – was gone.

The person sitting across from me was a monster wearing my Father's face.

Hot tears blurred my vision as they spilled from my eyes, streaming down my cheeks and dropping off my chin.

"Dad." I took in a trembling breath, trying hard to push away my fear and grief. I needed to reach him somehow, to find the sweet Man under the cruel mask. He had to be in there somewhere. "I love you. Please, don't do this. I love you!"

He squinted, and suddenly his eyes were blue and slightly bloodshot.

Professor Greyson.

"No," he said. The glasses disappeared, and he stared down the barrel of the gun at me. His voice was as smooth and calm as ever. "You don't, Laura. You only think you do."

Then he pulled the trigger, and my world blew apart.

* * *

I jerked awake, a scream tearing from my throat.

"Jesus! Keep her quiet!"

Before I could process where I was, a large body rolled over mine and a rough-skinned hand covered my mouth. My shriek died in a inaudible whimper, and I fought against the body pinning me down, jerking and kicking.

"Hey, Laura, it's okay! It's just me. It's okay!"

The whispered words infiltrated my brain, and I blinked up at a pair of beautiful grey-blue eyes.

Damon.

My muscles relaxed slightly. It was stupid; I had no reason to trust this man, or any of his friends. But with the horror of my dream still lingering on the edges of my mind, I needed something to cling to. I trembled, letting out a broken sob, and the large man sat up, bringing me with him and wrapping his arms around me.

"It's okay, Laura. We've got you. It was just a bad dream. We've all had them."

He continued to murmur a stream of comforting words into my ear, and I let him rock me gently until my heart rate slowed and my breathing evened out. As I grew calmer, I became uncomfortably aware of how much of our bodies were touching — and memories of the last time he'd touched me flooded my mind.

I wasn't uncomfortable with my body. I'd been sick for so long I was used to being poked and prodded by doctors, used to clinical stares. But I wasn't used to hands that touched me like I was a person, eyes that grew heated when they looked at me.

Clearing my throat, I pulled away from the blond man's embrace. He released me easily, and I scrambled back a few feet, kneeling on the soft ground beneath the canopy of the tarp as my gaze flicked back and forth between him and the tall man called Jack. Early morning light pierced the branches of the trees in the forest, dappling the ground with speckles of yellow.

"Damon." My voice sounded scratchy, and I tried to wipe away my tears and sniffles in a subtle movement—not like they did not know I had just been crying. "What... what is going on? Who are you?"

He grimaced slightly, looking a little sheepish. "Well, first of all, my name isn't Damon. It's Noah."

I blinked. "What?"

"Damon was the name I gave Hound when they hired me. I had a whole fake ID set up for their background checks and stuff."

"Noah," I repeated slowly, fighting the urge not to freak out.

This shouldn't be the thing that tipped me over the edge of sanity. Of all the strange events in the past twenty-four hours, this didn't even make the top ten. But why couldn't *anything* I believed stay constant for more than a few hours anymore?

I turned to the other man. "And what's *your* real name?"

He grinned, his full lips spreading wide over shiny white teeth. His features were beautiful, almost impossibly even, and two dimples graced his cheeks.

"It's still Jack. Noah was the only one who went in undercover, so he's the only one who got an alias."

"I don't understand. Went in undercover? Why? What were you doing at the Hound Facility? Why did you kidnap me?" I paused, realizing that although I was cold and sore, I basically felt okay. "How did you treat me? Do you have medicine?"

Damon—*Noah*—shook his head. "Nah., I mean, I think we have some painkillers in one of these packs. But you don't need medicine, Laura. I told you, you're not sick."

Jesus. Men.

I became erect. "You're going to tell me whether I'm sick or not? Do you realize how messed up that is? I've been dealing with Speyer's Disease since I was a kid, I think I would know—"

"You're not sick. You're an experiment."

His quiet voice cut off my rant. The word *experiment* pierced my heart, spreading a dull ache in my chest. I had always worried about being seen only as my illness, as nothing but a walking medical mystery.

"No. I'm more than that. Professor Greyson said they're all invested in my recovery. They want to see me get better."

"They want to see you shift," Jack threw out, raising one eyebrow.

I blinked. "Shift?"

Instead of elaborating, he turned to *Noah*. "Her vampire gift hasn't been called yet?"

Noah scrubbed a hand through his hair, sitting back on his heels and regarding me. "No, not yet. They were doing something different with her. It was a smaller operation, fewer test subjects. They didn't talk much around me, since I was just an attendant, but they were all really interested in her progress. You saw how it was—that whole complex existed just to house a few subjects. And she was definitely their most promising one."

Anger and fear flooded inside me, making me strangely bold.

"I'm not a fucking test subject! My name is Laura Maddow, and I'm a human being."

The two men exchanged a glance I couldn't interpret before Jack looked back at me. "Yeah... that's not exactly true anymore."

"What. Are. You. Talking. About?"

I couldn't tell if they were giving me half-answers because they thought I couldn't handle whatever they had to say, or if they were intentionally trying to keep me in the dark.

All I knew was that I needed someone to say something that made sense before I completely lost my shit.

I wasn't sure anymore what was going on at the Hound Facility. I didn't know what had happened to my Father, why he had turned on me — and that wound was still so raw it hurt to even think about. And I didn't understand how I'd been outside for almost twenty-four hours, tromping through woods and streams, no less, yet seemed to be in okay health.

Jack must've read the look on my face, because he dropped the kid gloves. His voice was a little harder when he spoke next, and he didn't couch his words or speak in riddles.

"The Hound Facility is a multi-billion-dollar biomedical research firm. For the past thirteen years, they've dedicated a large part of their operation to a secret project: creating shifters. People who are part human, part animal, able to take the form of both. They haven't perfected it yet. We don't know what they're trying to accomplish with this in the long-term, but they're still running tests. The facility you were in? All the 'patients' who were there? You were all a special batch of experiments."

I wanted to laugh. But the look on his face was so serious, his tone so sombre, that I couldn't. So I didn't say anything. I just stared at him, as though if I waited long enough, maybe he'd take it all back.

Noah dipped his head to the side, catching my gaze. "It's true, Laura. We all came from another, now non-operational facility near San Diego.

We escaped a while back, and eventually they shut down that branch. But they didn't stop experimenting. Why would they? They're playing god, and it's working."

Finally, a small, incredulous laugh did burst from my throat. "No! That's crazy! I'm sick. I'm not an... an *animal*. I've never *shifted* in my life. That's fantasy stuff!"

"Yeah, but that doesn't mean it's not true." Noah's large fingers dug lightly into the dirt by his side as he regarded me. "That night you seized? That was the shift starting to happen. Like I said, they did something different to you. A different dose, maybe a different cocktail of drugs? I'm not sure. But your change is coming. They were all really excited about it—that it was finally happening. I don't think anyone else at that complex survived their first shift."

A drip of fear dripped down my spine as I remembered the other patients who'd been housed at the Hound Facility with me. Now that I thought about it, I realized I'd been the longest-term resident there. Others had come and gone; I'd been told some of them got better and some of them didn't.

But if what these men were saying was true, none of them had been sick.

And none of them had gotten better.

They'd all died.

My throat stiffened. I couldn't keep letting panic get the best of me like this, but I felt like I was trapped in a rushing river, smashing into rocks and boulders as I careened helplessly toward a fate I couldn't see or understand.

Disbelief warred with a growing, grim certainty.

Even if these men were lying, I could no longer deny one truth. Something had been very wrong at the Hound Facility. I hadn't seen it because I hadn't wanted to—I'd been so focused on my hope for the future, on following Professor Greyson's orders so that my body could heal itself.

I hadn't seen it because the one person I thought I could trust more than anyone, my Father, had showed up every week to reassure me. He had placed absolute faith in the Hound Facility and had urged me to do the same.

The enormity of the betrayal, of the lies that had surrounded me every minute of every day for the past eight years of my life, suddenly bore down on me like a thousand pounds of rubble. I leaned over, going to my hands and knees, and retched into the grass. I hadn't eaten anything since before my check up with Professor Greyson yesterday—an event that seemed to have taken place in another lifetime—so all that flew out of my mouth was bile and spit.

Instead of yelling at me for barfing inside their little shelter, the two men sat sympathetically, letting me heave until my stomach was completely empty.

My dark brown hair fell down around my face like a curtain, and as I gathered it up with a shaking hand, I felt Noah's hand on my back.

"I'm sorry, Laura. We didn't come there for you, but when I saw you in that hall, so scared and alone, I couldn't just leave you there. None of us could. Maybe it would've been kinder to let you live the lie a little while longer. But you would've found out eventually. Once you finally shifted, the life you were living would've been over."

I closed my eyes, trying to calm my racing heart as his words washed over me. My stomach still churned, but there was nothing left inside it. My heart felt just as empty too. I'd spent the past eight years living a simple, isolated life. Even though I hadn't had much, I'd convinced myself I had everything I needed.

But I never truly had anything. And now I have even less than that.

In a moment of painful, striking clarity, I realized the three men who had stolen me away from the Hound Facility were now my only lifeline in a world that loomed too large and dangerous to understand.

Blowing out a deep breath, I sat back, lifting my head. Noah's face was close to mine, his cloud-gray eyes dark with concern.

"You said…" I licked my dry lips. "You said *shifters.* Part human, part animal. What does that mean?"

He opened his mouth to reply, but movement in the sunlight-dappled woods caught his attention.

As if called by our voices, two vampires prowled through the trees toward us.

Chapter 9 -Vampires Shift

They wore the same fangs on their teeth.

I'd always assumed vampires were afraid of sunlight. Not that I'd seen many of either, except for in movies or TV shows. But these vampires were different, with their skins radiantly glowing under the sun without a single burn and the fact they looked like werewolves, I guessed they were hybrids. One was familiar; the other looked like he had been on his own for too long.

They padded closer, dipping their heads to sniff the ground. The familiar one with amber eyes looked right at me, and I found myself deep-rooted to the spot. There was something intelligent and assessing—almost human—in his gaze.

Jack and Noah seemed a bit less concerned, Marcus had run off alone and now was arriving with a newbie that looked bushed. They didn't flinch as Marcus and the newbie slipped inside the makeshift shelter.

I'd seen nature shows where rabbits or other prey animals froze in place when they sensed a predator, and I'd never understood where that instinct came from. But I understood it now. My body was rooted to the spot, torn between conflicting impulses to run, hide, or fight.

The newbie let out a shriek, and then...

He changed.

His entire body seemed to ripple. Fangs shifted beneath his tooth, changing size and shape. His nails retreated, vanishing into his body until only lightly tanned nails remained. Dark hair grew on his head as his face transformed from the ugly vampire and werewolf skin that registered on his face to that of a man.

The black-haired man named Marcus. The one who'd run off the previous night.

Beside him, the fatigued newbie shuddered as well, and even before the change was about to get complete, My mind pondered on where Marcus had gotten him from and definitely who he was.

Vampire shifters. That was all I knew, they were shifters.

My mind reeled. I'd seen the change occur right before my eyes, and I still could scarcely believe it. Jack and Noah hadn't lied to me — about any of it.

The three of them and the newbie were vampire shifters.

And at the moment, two of them were also completely, bare-ass naked.

My fear at being approached by two predators splintered into a thousand other emotions. Shock. Awe.

Embarrassment.

Neither of the men paused in their stride or made any effort to cover their nudity. Jack walked over to one of the packs that leaned against a tree-trunk, while Marcus came to a stop in front of me.

I tried. I did. I really and truly tried not to glare at the thick piece of muscle that hung between his legs, but since I was sitting on the ground, it was basically at my eye level. And the harder I tried not to look, the more my eyes seemed to bug out of my head.

"What? You've never seen a naked man before?" Marcus cocked a challenging eyebrow at me.

No. As a matter of fact, I hadn't. I knew it was late in life to have missed out on something like that, but I'd never even been kissed, let alone gotten to second, third, or fourth base.

But I'd be damned if I was going to admit that to him. I was off-centre, wholly uncertain about where my life was going to take me from here on out. But one thing I felt sure of was that I couldn't let these men think they were better or tougher than me. I couldn't let them think I was weak. Couldn't let them know how inexperienced I was in so many ways.

"It's not that." I moved my gaze up to his face before deliberately dropping it back down to his dick again. "I've just never seen one this small."

There was a moment of stunned silence as Noah stopped digging through the bag by the tree. Then all three of the other men howled with laughter. I smirked, relishing my victory and somehow pleased to have eased the mood in the camp.

Or at least, some people's moods.

Marcus's blue eyes chilled, and he raked his gaze over my body, taking in my shirt and pants. Sometime while I was asleep, the guys had put the socks and boots on me too. They were a little snug, but I'd take pinched toes over numb ones any day.

"Nice clothes," he said in a hard voice.

Noah's laughter died out. "Hey, I'm sorry, Marcus. But wherever Luke is, he'd want Laura to have them. You know that."

Marcus didn't answer. Sadness flitted across his features, almost as acute as I'd seen last night. Did he carry this pain everywhere with him? All the time?

Brushing his black curls away from his face, he turned away from me and joined Damon by the tree. The two men stepped into fresh sets of clothes, then Jack pulled out two pairs of boots, tossing one to Marcus and the newbie that stood confused.

Compassion tugged at my heart. Whatever grief he carried, I could understand it. My wounds were still fresh, but I had a feeling they would never stop hurting.

"I'm sorry." I hugged my arms around myself. "I don't know who Luke is, but... I'm sorry I'm here instead of him."

"It's fine."

Marcus's voice didn't match his words at all, and he wouldn't look at me.

I tried again. "Whoever he is, I'm grateful to him."

"Luke's his brother. He was held at the same complex we were in—" Jack began, but Marcus turned on him with a growl.

"Don't talk about him! *She*"—he pointed his hands to me, lip curling—"don't need to know."

Jack heaved a sigh, flopping down on the ground and leaning against the tree trunk to tie his boots. "Come on, man. Don't be a dick."

"I'm not being a dick," Marcus ground out. "And this is not part of our plan. It isn't anywhere close to the plan. We should've gotten Luke out and been halfway to New York by now."

"Yeah, but he wasn't there," Jack countered. "So that part of the plan was already shot. What were we supposed to do?"

"Not pick up some stray who's only going to slow us the fuck down! We need to start planning a new strategy. We need to go back!"

Jack scrubbed at his short black hair. "He's not there, Marcus."

"Then I'll find out where he is! And I'll get him out myself if I fucking have to."

The other three men shared a look, and I had a feeling they'd had this conversation, or something like it, many times before. Marcus didn't seem like the type of man who gave up on an idea easily. And he clearly didn't give up on someone he loved easily.

I would've appreciated those qualities, if I didn't already sort of hate the moody, coldly handsome man.

"You won't have to do that alone," Jack said finally. "We're with you, brother. Always."

He stood, coming eye-to-eye with Marcus. All the men towered over me, but those two were the tallest. Jack had slightly broader shoulders than Marcus, and even through his long-sleeved shirt, I could see his muscles rippling as he moved. His left sleeve was torn and streaked with blood from where the bullet had grazed him.

"He's right." Noah stood, stretching out his hand and helping me to my feet too. Jack rose too, grumbling something about having just sat down. "We're with you. But we can't go back there. My cover is blown. They know all of our faces. Hell, they probably have hunters out searching for us right now. We can't just run back into the belly of the beast. We need to regroup, reorganize. And we need more backup."

"What? *Her*?" Marcus shot me a scathing look.

"My name's Laura, not *her*. And what do you say about him" I pulled out my hands from Noah's. It was too comforting, and I couldn't allow myself to think of any of these men as my protectors, no matter how tempting it was. I pointed to the newbie at least I thought he was "And don't worry, I won't burden you. I'll..."

I trailed off. What the hell *would* I do?

I had no idea where I was. No hint on how to navigate the world outside the Hound Facility. Especially not on the run. And especially not as a... shifter.

"No way, Laura. We got you out of that place. What kind of assholes would we be if we just abandoned you now?" Jack grinned, raising a pointed eyebrow at the black-haired shifter next to him. "And Norman isn't a newbie, he's one of us" he pointed to the newbie who leaned on a tree's bark. "We needed someone to watch over our stuff when we attacked the facility and Norman volunteered".

Marcus's stormy blue eyes still narrowed, but he had the decency to look a little ashamed.

"You can come with us," he said reluctantly, and I had to bite my lip to keep me from throwing the offer back in his face. As angry as he had made me, I couldn't afford to roam off on my own in a hurry.

Instead, I nodded, lowering my eyes. "Okay."

"That still leaves the question, where the hell are we going?" Jack cocked his head, staring off into the woods and listening attentively.

The movement was so animalistic that for a moment, I vividly remembered the vampire shifter who'd padded into the makeshift enclosure a few minutes ago. It was still there, under the surface of Jack's skin. I never would've noticed or believed it if I hadn't just seen him shift, but now that I knew it to be real; I could sense the animal inside him.

Was something like that really inside me too? Right now, I almost wished it were true. I longed for the strength of an apex predator, the instincts and power of a vampire shifter.

But all I could sense inside myself at the minute was a very petrified, very confused human.

"I dunno, but we need to get moving soon." Noah followed Jack's gaze, his large, warm hand enveloping mine again. "I don't know how many resources Hound will dedicate to hunting us, but that blond Terminator dude definitely looked like he meant business. And the fact that we stole their prize experiment..." He looked back at me, a surprisingly protective glint in his eyes. "Yeah, they'll be coming after us."

My stomach dipped. Less than twenty-four hours ago, I would've been delighted to return to the Hound Facility. But now? A shiver of dread raced down my spine at the prospect.

"What about the Lost Pack?" Jack hefted a large backpack over his shoulder, his dark eyes serious.

"We don't even know they exist. It could just be a rumour." Marcus looked torn between hope and despair.

"What's... the Lost Pack?" My voice was soft. I was half-afraid Marcus would bite my head off again.

But he surprised me by turning to me and answering, his tone less openly unfriendly than it had been before. "The Hound Corporation has been doing experiments on humans for years. When they started the shifter initiative, I don't think they really knew what to expect. Their security wasn't nearly as good as it should've been, bearing in mind what they created. In the early days, a lot of the shifters escaped, and rumour has it, a group of them formed a pack in the Pacific Northwest." He shifted his gaze to Jack. "But we don't know if it's true."

"Hey, man. Beats the fuck outta sitting around here waiting for Hound to come after us. And who'd be more likely to help us bust your brother out than shifters who've escaped themselves? They'll understand better than anybody." Norman rocked on his feet, practically bouncing on his toes.

"That makes sense to me," I said tentatively.

I barely understood what was going on, and I doubted I'd get a vote in any of this. But Norman's restless energy was rubbing off on me, and I was anxious to get moving. My gaze kept darting into the woods as if at any moment, I'd catch a glimpse of bright blond hair and hulking muscle.

Marcus regarded me so intensely it felt like he was trying to read my mind, to strip away all my defences and see right down to my soul. His eyes were a shocking blue, brighter than Noah's, like an infinitely bright blue sky.

I didn't blink, didn't look away, as his gaze devoured me.

"Is that what you want, Laura?" He called out my name for the first time, but it sounded different rolling off his tongue. Less loving and more like a quiet threat. "You want to meet more of your kind? More people like us?"

My heart was beating too hard in my chest. How did he—how did *all* of these men—put me off balance so quickly? I felt like a bumbling idiot around them, awkward and unsure.

But I nodded, forcing my chin up and down. "Yes. I do." I dilly-dallied, then added, "And if they might be able to help get your brother back, that's a chance worth taking, right?"

He ran a hand through his wavy black hair. It'd been tied back in a low ponytail yesterday, but now the ends of the dark Hounds brushed his shoulders. Finally, he nodded conclusively.

"Like Laura says, it's worth a shot."

"Exactly what I said! Now quit eye-fucking her, and let's go." Jack swiped a bag from the ground and set off through the forest, his laugh lingering behind him.

I flushed all the way from my toes to the tips of my ears, and to my surprise, Marcus's cheeks reddened a little too. He tore his gaze away from me, bending down to pick up the pack Jack had pulled Luke's clothes from yesterday. He tossed the bag in my direction, and I hastily untied my hand from Noah's so I could catch it before it hit me in the chest. Noah made a sound low in his throat, almost like a growl, but Marcus ignored him.

"If you're coming with us, you're gonna have to pull your own weight, Laura. No free rides here. This isn't a fucking vacation," he said, before taking hold of a pack of his own and heading off after Jack.

And just like that, I was back to detesting the moody asshole.

Chapter 10 -Finding the Lost Pack

I stared after Marcus's retreating form, a riot of emotions banging around in my chest.

"Here, Laura. Let me help you."

Noah tried to take the bag from me, but I held onto it with an iron grip. "No! That's okay."

It was the same size as all the others and unexpectedly heavy, but I refused to let Marcus be right about me—I wouldn't be a burden or a freeloader. I shoved my arms through the straps and hefted the backpack higher on my shoulders, following after Norman and Jack. They trailed behind Marcus, hanging back to wait for us.

I hoped at least one of these guys knew where we were going, because I certainly didn't. I had a unclear idea that east was behind us, where the sun soared low on the horizon, but that was about all the sense of direction I possessed.

As we caught up to the two men, they parted to make room, and I found myself walking between them.

Jack shot me a look out of the corner of his eye. "So, you must have about a million questions, huh?"

I thought about that for a second as we tromped through the underbrush. I did have questions, but there were so many it was hard to express any of them. And there were several I wasn't sure I was ready to hear the answers to. But if he was offering information, I shouldn't waste this chance.

"Yeah." I looked up at him, looking against the morning light. "I guess I do have."

"Then ask away. I'm an open book." He grinned. His nose had definitely been broken before, and with the teasing tilt of his lips, he looked dangerously handsome and wild.

I ripped my gaze away from his face before he could catch me gazing, uttering out the first question that popped into my mind. "Does it hurt when you shift?"

He swept a low-hanging branch out of the way, pursing his lips thoughtfully. "A little. It hurt more the first few times, but now I'm just used to it. It's like if you crack your knuckles over and over—eventually you don't really feel it at all."

That didn't help calm my fears. One of the nurses at the Hound Facility had cracked her knuckles, and the sound had always made me cringe.

"For long have you been able to do shift?"

He cocked his head. "I shifted for the first time when I was eleven."

My brows shot up, and I almost twisted my ankle as I turned to look up at him. "Eleven? How old are you now?"

"Twenty-six."

"Fifteen years." I drew the words out slowly. He was four years older than me, and he'd been shifting for over a decade. If these men were right, and I was also a subject of the Hound's experiments, why hadn't I shifted once yet? Brushing off my sudden worry that there *was* something wrong with me, I glanced at Norman. "What about you?"

"My first shift? When I was fourteen."

"When did you escape Hound?"

Jack glanced over my head to meet Norman's eyes before answering. "Six years ago. We all escaped together—the four of us. Been together ever since."

The look they shared made a sharp pain flicker in my chest. It was just a casual glance, but it spoke of family, brotherhood, and love. I couldn't imagine what they'd been through in the past six years, or what they'd experienced before that either. But whatever it was, it had cemented the bond between all four of them more deeply than even blood could.

I wished I had something like that.

"I can't believe my dad just gave me up to the Hound Corporation like that," I muttered, realizing only after the words were out of my mouth that I'd spoken my deepest hurt aloud. My voice wavered as I fought to keep it under control. "He went along with everything they said, told me they'd take care of me. But...he knew. The whole time, he knew."

Jack leaned toward me slightly, bumping my arm with his in an affectionate gesture. The brightness of his amber eyes dimmed a little as he looked down at me. "I hate to tell you this, Laura, but that Man probably wasn't your Father."

My foot caught on a root, and I staggered several steps, almost falling forward onto the soft ground. Jack caught my elbow, steadying me.

"He… he wasn't?" I whispered, my steps slowing.

Some part of me had realized that the moment he'd shot at me. Even if he had been my Father by blood, he was no longer a dad in any of the ways that counted.

Not if he could look me in the eye and aim a gun at me.

Maybe knowing he wasn't my real dad should've been reassuring—but it wasn't. It didn't change the fact that I'd loved him for as long as I could remember. It didn't change the fact that he'd lied to me my entire life. And it didn't change the fact that my real parents, whoever they were, had given me up somewhere along the line.

"No." It was Norman who answered, his hand on me tightening slightly as he spoke. "He was a Hound employee. They probably bought you on the black market or snatched you from the foster system when you were little. That's how they got most of the younger test subjects in our complex. Some of the older ones were homeless. People no one would miss."

"That's awful."

My stomach twisted with pity, until I realized I was also one of those people no one would miss.

"Yeah." Norman's voice was hard as glass. "It is."

"But... I don't seem understand." I shook my head, adjusting the straps of the backpack slightly on my shoulders as I walked. The straps were starting to dig in, the weight of the bag bearing down hard on my back, but I pushed the discomfort away. "Why? Why go to all that trouble? I lived at the Hound Facility for years. Since I was eleven. All my memories from before I got there are vague, but I always thought that was because I was sick all the time. They must've done something to make me forget."

"Seems likely. It wouldn't be that hard, with the kind of pharmaceuticals they have access to." Jack nodded.

"But *why*?" I insisted. "That was such an elaborate setup, just to make me think I belonged there. Why do all that for me?"

"Because you're special, Laura," Noah said from behind me. "Something about you is unlike, and important."

"Yeah, they didn't do all those bells and whistles for us," Jack added, his voice tinged with anger. "They treated us like fucking dogs."

Special.

They'd used that word before. But I didn't feel special.

I felt alone, unwanted, and unloved.

Tears stung my eyes, burning hot trails down my cheeks. I blinked quickly but didn't reach up to wipe them away. I didn't want to draw attention to the fact that I was crying. I didn't want to them to see me as weak as I felt.

If the guys noticed, they didn't say anything, giving me time to process my grief privately. We lapsed into silence after that, the quiet stillness of the forest broken only by the crunch of our feet on the ground. With every step I took, I could feel myself getting farther and farther away from the life I knew.

I was walking into a great unknown, a vast, uncharted territory, and fear of the future felt like a lead weight around my ankles, making every step drag.

The backpack grew heavier and heavier on my back too. I wasn't in bad shape, thanks to the routine Ernie — or whatever the fuck her real name was — had created for me. But I wasn't used to being outside, wasn't used to working on too little sleep with too little food and water. The one break we took at midday was hardly enough to restore my fading strength.

Don't be the weak link, Laura. Don't give them a cause to leave you behind.

Those words became like a song over the next few hours, repeated over and over in my head as I forced one foot in front of the next — tripping over roots and rocks more often as my strength and coordination faded. But none of the men surrounding me showed any signs of tiring. So I clenched my teeth and kept going.

Until I couldn't anymore.

A wave of gray crept over my vision, and I pitched forward, landing on my hands and knees. My backpack slipped to one side, and the weight almost dragged me over. I dug my fingers into the dirt, fighting the dizziness that threatened to overpower me.

"Shit! Laura, are you okay?" Noah's face swam in my vision, his stormy blue eyes worried.

"Uh huh. I'm fine," I slurred, unconvincingly.

"Should've carried the damn pack myself," he chastised under his breath, helping me sit up and tugging the backpack off my shoulders. I suddenly felt so light I thought I might float away.

"What's wrong with her?" Marcus stood over me.

I hauled myself to my feet, the movement way too fast. I almost fell again. He reached out to catch me, but before he could touch me, I staggered away.

"Nothing. I'm okay." My voice sounded stronger this time. Pride and anger were giving my body the shot of adrenaline it needed. I would *not* allow Marcus to help me.

"Bullshit, you're fine." Noah picked up my pack, slinging one strap over his shoulder as if the combined weight of two bags was nothing. He turned to Marcus. "She's not used to this. She's still basically fucking human, not to mention she's been living inside a bunker. Shit, her vampire shift hasn't even been called yet. We can't just expect her to keep up with us. She needs a break."

"Goddamnit!" Marcus stalked a few paces away before coming back to stand in front of us. He clenched his hands into fists, and I noticed his knuckles were tight and every expression of anger were written all over it.

"I fucking knew it! It's already happening. We're already altering everything for her! This isn't a fucking Disney cruise, and if she wanted it easy, she shouldn't have—"

"What?" Noah's voice was quiet. "Been abducted by Hound? Had her entire life stolen from her? Been ripped away from everything she thought she knew? None of us signed up for this, Marcus. All of us got a raw fucking deal. Remember that, or when we finally find Luke, you won't be the brother he deserves."

Marcus stared at him, his jaw set. He swallowed hard, but didn't speak.

"We need to stop sometime soon, anyway," Jack put in. "We've gotta snag a new ride. No harm in getting a little sleep while we're at it. It's a long way to New York State."

New York.

I wrapped my arms around myself as I processed his words. That was our final destination. Where the mysterious and possibly non-existent "Lost Pack" lived.

And I was headed there with four men I barely knew. One of whom obviously hated me, and none of whom I was certain I could trust.

Chapter 11-New Family

With a little more prodding from the other three.

Marcus finally agreed it was a good idea to stop. I celebrated inwardly while remaining outwardly indifferent. The truth was, I wasn't sure how much farther I could go before I fell over and couldn't get up again.

Fortunately, we weren't as far from civilization as I'd thought. Noah carried my pack as we walked through the woods for another mile or so before emerging onto a small, two-lane road. Another ten minute walk led us into a small town that looked like its heyday had been several decades ago. Half the shops seemed to be closed up, and the paint on most of the buildings were washed-out and peeling. But I didn't care. The hotel on the outskirts of town had a sign out front that read "Vacancy," and I could already feel the softness of a pillow against my cheek, the comfort of a roof over my head.

"We shouldn't all go in," Jack said as we walked down the quiet street toward the hotel. "If four guys and a girl check into one room in a middle-of-nowhere hotel like this, they're definitely gonna think something shady is going on."

"We'll both go." Jack grabbed me by the elbow, pulling me toward him. "You guys go get us some food."

The others nodded, splitting off silently. I wondered if their attempt at keeping a low profile was pointless. All four of these men were distractingly handsome, and in a small town like this, I was sure we stood out whether we wanted to or not. But I didn't voice my concern as Jack led me toward the old hotel. It was a two-story structure with a small parking lot out front. An office sat in the centre, with two wings extended out and back from there. Room numbers were tacked to each of the doors.

Jack opened the door for me, gesturing me inside the small, dingy office. There was a coffee maker on a little table set near one wall, with a half a pot of what smelled like very burnt coffee sitting abandoned inside it. Old magazines were placed in a loose stack nearby.

No one was behind the counter, but when the door slammed shut too hard between us, a voice called out.

"Coming!"

A middle-aged man with a trucker hat shoved over shoulder-length brown hair stepped out from the back room and rested on the counter with both elbows.

"Hey there, folks. What can I do for you?"

"We need a room for the night," Jack answered, stepping up beside me.

The hotel clerk swept his gaze over the two of us, letting it linger on me. His thick tongue darted out to lick his lips as he cocked his head.

I'd gotten used to being poked, prodded, and observed at the Hound Facility, where it was an almost daily occurrence. But no one had *ever* looked at me the way this man was staring at me now.

I detested it.

It made my skin crawl—made me feel helpless and dirty, even though I couldn't quite tell why.

The man tossed his stringy brown hair over his shoulder, smiling at me. "A room for the night, huh? What kind?"

"Double." Jack's voice sounding deeper and more convincing, and when I looked over at him, I saw his jaw tighten.

The man seemed pleased by that answer for some reason. "Huh. Not a single? Can't quite close the deal?" He winked at me. "You need a real man, honey? You just come find me."

He chuckled, still running his gaze up and down my body, as if he had every right to stare at any part of me he wanted for as long as he wanted. I quivered. I wanted to step back, to cower behind Jack. But the same instinct that had made me stand up to Marcus kept me still now.

Fuck that. I wouldn't run. I wouldn't let this man think he had power over me.

Jack's arm slid around my waist, his large hand resting gently on my hip. He didn't look at me though. His eyes were locked on the ogling desk clerk, and I could practically feel the anger burning through him.

"You heard what I said. We need a double. One night. How much?"

The man's attention went to my side, where Jack's hand curled possessively around my body. Then he flicked his gaze up to meet Jack's, his lip curling. "Sixty."

"Fine."

Jack pulled me forward, keeping his arm around me. He reached into his back pocket with his free hand and pulled out a small stack of bills. With a loud thunk, he slapped them on the counter. I had stiffened when he first drew me into his side, but now I shyly returned the gesture, slipping my arm around his waist under the pack strapped to his back. It felt a little strange, and I wasn't sure where to put my hand. Finally, I reached around his front with my other arm and clasped hands, circling Jack in the world's most awkward hug.

The slimy desk clerk frowned, then rolled his eyes and grabbed the cash off the counter, turning to the wall behind him to grab a key card labelled 25. He chucked it toward Jack, then collected the—false—name the room would be rented under.

Finally, Jack directed me toward the exit, only releasing me from his grasp to open the door for me again.

We took a right and went up the stairs, following the upper walkway toward our rented room.

"Thank you for that," I murmured.

"No problem. You must get creeps like him staring at you all the time."

I huffed out a cheerless laugh. "Actually, no. He was the first. The doctors at the Hound Facility might be mad scientists, but at least they never stared at me like that."

Jack's easy stride hitched, and he looked down at me with a grimace.

"Oh, shit. Right. I'm sorry." We got to the room, and he put in the key card into the lock. "Out here, it's probably going to happen a lot. With the way you look? Creeps will come out of the fucking woodwork for sure."

With the way I looked?

I'd never considered myself particularly striking. I'd had a full-length mirror in my room at the Hound Facility, and I'd sometimes stood in front of it, examining my naked body as though searching for weaknesses. Places where my illness might attack.

My legs and arms were toned and my stomach flat thanks to my work with Ernie. I had a small, elfin nose that came to a delicate point, a heart shaped face, and high cheekbones. I'd always thought my eyes were my best feature—although now, remembering how closely my "dad's" had seemed to match them, I sort of hated the rich amber colour.

I knew what all the distinct parts of me looked like, but I'd never really well thought-out what they all added up to. What my appearance was like to an outside eye.

A flush rose in my cheeks as I remembered the way Jack himself had looked at me the night before, when he'd helped me out of my hospital gown and into dry clothes. The way his gaze had slipped just for a half-second to take in the bare skin of my breasts. The hotness in his eyes when he'd looked back at my face.

But the look he'd worn then hadn't been anything like the look the hotel clerk had on his face. It hadn't made my skin crawl. Instead, it had sparked a small fire inside my belly that still seemed to burn low, flaring with sudden heat every time Jack touched me or looked at me with his deep brown eyes.

The hotel room door swung open, and for a moment, we just stood outside it. Jack's hand relaxed on the handle, but he made no move to enter the room. I was sure he could read every emotion on my face, and I tried to push down the blood colouring my cheeks by sheer force of will as I broke away from his gaze and stepped inside.

"This is nice."

I looked around the small room. The carpet was aggressively orange, and chintzy watercolour paintings decorated the walls. Two large beds sat a few feet apart against one wall, and the rest of the space was mostly bare.

Jack chuckled. "No, it isn't. You really have been locked up too long, haven't you?"

The heat in my cheeks grew. "Yeah, I guess so."

I sat on the bed while Jack let go of his bag and prowled around the room. He checked the bathroom then switched on the lights and tugged the curtains on the window closed. He rested casually against the wall between the door and the window, sneaking a quick look out through the space between the curtain and the frame.

The room was quiet for a few minutes before the silence began to grate on me. I'd been used to days passing with little or no discussion at the Hound Facility, but everything was different out here.

Silence was no longer soothing like it had once been. Now it was laden with millions of unsaid things.

"Is Marcus okay?" I uttered.

Jack's eyes met mine, their dark depths soft and mysterious.

"Yeah, he will be." He crossed his arms over his chest, the muscles of his biceps huddling and bulging. "We had to leave his younger brother, Luke, behind when we escaped the compound, we were all being held in. He told him to go—*pleaded with* him to—but he's been fucked up about it ever since, as you can see."

I bit my lip, pity for the ice-cold man filling my chest.

"He was so sure Luke was in that facility where we found you." Jack rubbed the back of his neck. "It hit him hard. Now he's bemoaning him loss all over again."

My stomach twisted. "But he's not gone, right? I mean, he's still alive somewhere?"

Jack's face was expressionless, but his voice was heavy. "We don't know."

His words settled between us, but before I could ask anything else, he whipped his head to the side, looking out the window again. He opened the door and waved outside, drawing the attention of the other three guys as they walked across the hotel's parking lot. They changed direction, turning toward the stairs.

When they were all inside the room, Norman kicked the door shut and slid the chain into place.

"We couldn't decide what to get, so we got some of everything." Noah dropped a plastic bag on the bed next to the one I was sitting on.

Norman imitated his movement, adding another bag and some bottles of water. "Yeah, we supersized the shit out of it."

The most inviting aroma I'd ever smelled drifted up to meet my nostrils, and drool pooled in the corner of my mouth. Without even noticing what I was doing, I stood and drifted over toward the other bed, staring at the large bags.

"Have you ever taken fast food, Laura?" Noah asked curiously.

I shook my head, chewing on my lower lip.

"You can pick first, then. Whatever you want. And there's plenty, so go nuts." He grinned and stepped back, pointing to the bed with a grand flourish.

I shot a quick look at all the guys. Everyone but Marcus nodded encouragingly. He possibly hated to see me getting special treatment again, but the echoing of my stomach urged me on despite his death glare.

Tentatively, like a squirrel sneaking up to a picnic, I crawled onto the soft mattress and reached into one of the bags. I didn't have the guts to ransack through it all, so I just grabbed the first thing I touched and opened it.

A hamburger. I knew that much, although I'd never eaten one before.

Holding it in both hands, I took a small bite.

My eyes bugged out. *Holy shit. So fucking good.*

I chewed in a hurry before going in for a second bite that was twice as big as the first. The burger wasn't huge, and after just a few more bites, it was gone. I hardly controlled myself from licking the paper it'd been wrapped in. Instead, I reached into the bag again and drew out a container of French fries, consuming them down too.

Then I had another burger. And another.

By the time I finished, I was pleasingly stuffed. I hadn't realized how hungry I was. And I hadn't known how fucking enjoyable fast food was.

I was licking the salt from the fries off each of my fingers when I finally came back to my senses and noticed the men were goggling at me. My heart stuttered in my chest, and I looked up, eyes wide.

"Shit! I'm sorry. Did I take too much?"

They all looked slightly shocked as they took in the carnage of empty wrappers around me. Their looks were a mixture of surprise, awe, and something else I couldn't quite pinpoint. Something that only made my blush deepen.

Then Jack laughed, the infectious sound breaking the tension.

"Fuck no! That was astonishing. I like a woman who isn't afraid to eat."

The other three chuckled, and I had a sudden wish to melt into the carpet. I scrambled off the bed, gesturing to the bags. "Er, I'm done."

The guys descended on the remaining food, polishing it off in short order — although none of them ate quite as much as I had.

I watched them talk and argue good-naturedly among themselves, pondering if I'd ever learn to act normal around these men. To become something more than a curiosity or an oddity to them.

And more importantly, I wondered why I cared.

Chapter 12-Caught Off Guard

I woke in a cold sweat. Pictures of my dad had permeated my dreams again, along with strange and twisted visions of the Hound Facility. Instead of being the safe haven I'd once seen it as, the walls in my dream had dripped with blood, and screams had echoed down the corridors as I was dragged into dark laboratories under the main building.

When my eyes popped open, a shout hovered on my lips. I choked it back, burying my face in the pillow as my body shook with concealed fear. The pillowcase was wet, I realized, soaked with tears I didn't remember crying.

I pulled the blanket over my head and lay curled up beneath it for a moment, trying to block out the world.

When my heart rate finally slowed, I raised the covers. The room was empty. With my belly full last night, I'd crawled into bed and passed out, fatigued from the long day. I hadn't even considered the sleeping arrangements, and as I looked around the gloomy room, guilt rose up in me.

Blankets had been torn off the other bed, possibly so some of the guys could sleep on the floor. They'd given me an entire bed to myself, and although I respected the gesture, I felt like a royal asshole.

Not that I want to share a bed with any of them, I reminded myself quickly. But I could've been the one to take the floor.

And where were they all now?

A sudden stab of fear pierced me. Were they gone? Had they decided Marcus was right about me being too much of a burden and left me here?

I sat up, holding the blanket to my body as my gaze scanned the room. Three of the packs were still here. The sight made my chest unclench just a little. They might leave me behind, but I seriously doubted they'd decisively leave without their stuff.

Pushing down my fear, I threw the covers off and shuffled over to the backpack I'd carried yesterday. There were more clothes in it, including brand new underwear and a bra they had bought when they had gone to get food the previous day. In fact, everything in the bag still had tags on them.

These things were all new, possibly bought by Noah in attempt to relieving my troubles. My guilt about putting on the clothes piled on top of the guilt about hogging the bed, and I felt about as tall as an inchworm as I headed toward the bathroom to shower.

The Hound Facility had been a prison in disguise, but it was still hard not to miss certain things about it. Like the shower. Particularly compared to this hotel's shitty shower, where huge droplets of water pelted me hard enough to sting, and the temperature knob balanced on a razor's edge between scalding and freezing. I spent the entire time adjusting the knob by eighths of an inch, and by the time I stepped out, my skin was pink from the wild temperature swings.

I threw on a fresh set of clothes and stepped out of the bathroom just as Noah and Jack returned.

"Oh, hey, Laura. You're up!"

Noah kicked the door shut behind them with his foot, smiling at me — the same smile that had knocked my socks off the first time I'd met him.

A lot had changed since then. I now knew his name was Noah, not Damon. I knew he was a vampire shifter, and I might be one too. In fact, my entire world had pretty much fallen down around my ears in the past few days.

But the effect his smile had on me were still the same.

My tongue immediately tied itself in knots, and I nodded awkwardly, settling onto the bed to roll up my old clothes and stuff them back into the bag.

"We brought some breakfast. Shit, I can't wait to see you decimate these," Jack teased, dropping a box of donuts on the bed.

Oh geez.

I was never going to live that down. Jack seemed to find my ravenous craving for new foods both funny and — shockingly — attractive.

I peeked into the box. It looked like it'd once held a dozen donuts, although there were fewer than that now. Faking nonchalance, I picked up a plain one dusted in cinnamon sugar and took a bite. Rich sweetness exploded on my tongue, and I worked hard to bite back a moan. The two men were already staring at me; I didn't want to make it any worse by adding pornographic noises.

To distract myself from taking down the entire pastry in two seconds, I looked up at them. "So, what's the plan? Where are you headed now?"

"*We are* headed to New York," Noah replied, emphasizing the word *we* as he made a gesture that encompassed me. "But we need to make a quick stop on the way. We have an old friend who might be able to help us. Norman and Marcus are picking up a car right now."

My brow furrowed, and I quietly snuck another donut. Somehow, despite my attempts at restraint, I'd finished the first one while Noah was speaking. "From where? Is there a car rental place in this town?"

"Oh, Laura." Jack smirked at me, dropping down onto the bed next to me and stretching out his long, muscular form. "They are not renting a car. They are stealing one dear."

I almost choked on my donut.

*Oh.*I shouldn't have been surprised to hear that. After all, these same men had broken into the Hound Facility two days ago and stolen something valuable from that place too — me.

But it was still hard to wrap my head around the fact that they were off stealing a car. It probably said a lot about how unworldly I was, but none of these guys fit what I imagined carjackers would look like.

Almost as if he could read my mind, Noah grinned at me. "Hey, when you're living under the radar, you take whatever work you can get. After we escaped the

Hound compound in San Diego, we fell in with a crew in Vegas. Learned a lot of useful skills on the jobs we did. Not all of them lawful," he said with a wink.

I found myself grinning back at him. My shock was beginning to fade, and for the first time since leaving Hound, I found myself feeling excited and a little hopeful. I didn't know if I'd ever get over the lies I'd been fed my entire life, but it was finally starting to sink in that I'd gotten the one thing I wanted most in the world: to *be in* the world.

This was real life, in all its messy, terrifying, unknowable glory. And as much as it sort of made me want to bury my head under the covers again, there was a part of me that relished it too. The bright chaos of the outside world was a constant reminder that I was alive.

That I was free.

That I'd made it this far.

"We all know how to hot wire a car. We could do it in our sleep. You didn't think the owner left the keys in that SUV yesterday, did you?" Jack raised his eyebrows at me, leaning over the bed to grab a donut from the box.

He had a pleasant sandalwood scent that tickled my nostrils, and the proximity of his body to mine made the little hairs on my arms stand up. I wasn't used to having other people this close, let alone such unnervingly handsome men, and it threw me off balance.

"It's not really a two person job, but it's easier if there's a lookout." He shrugged. "Safer too. I'm sure the Hound Corporation is still trying to find us, and if we have to split up the pack, it's better to do it two-by-two than to send anyone off on their own."

I toyed with the second half of my third donut. "Clutch. Right. That's what you guys are. It's so strange; I saw it with my own eyes, but I can still hardly believe it's true. You're... wolves."

"You'll get used to it." Noah shrugged. "Especially once your vampire gift is called. When you can shift too, it'll seem as natural as anything."

I nodded, although I was a little doubtful of that. "I guess so."

Jack shoved the last bite of food into his mouth. "Wanna see it again?"

My heart stuttered in my chest. "What? Your shifts?"

"Yeah." He smiled mischievously, looking over my head at Noah, who stayed on the other side of the bed. "What do you say? Do we show her?"

Noah ran a hand through his spiky blond hair. "I don't know, Jack. In a hotel room?"

"Aw, what difference does it make? Sure, it's not as impressive to see a shift in a hotel room as out in their element, but whatever. The lady hardly got a chance to see what she's in for. Let's show her."

Noah sighed. I got the impression Jack was the instigator and troublemaker of the group, but at the moment, I was completely on his side. When he and Marcus had come back to camp the other day and shifted, I'd been in such a state of shock that I'd hardly been able to take in the details of their vampire forms. And as frightening as it was to think of being trapped in a small hotel room with two large, vampire shifters, my curiosity overrode my nerves.

"Come on, Noah." My gaze met his, my teeth holding slightly my lip. "Please?"

Something shifted in his grey-blue eyes. His expression softened, and I knew he was going to give in because I had requested for it.

That thought delighted me way more than it should have. I was trying to keep up some level of barrier between myself and the four men who had rushed into my life two days ago. But the walls I put up kept falling. It was hard not to let these men take centre stage in my life and my mind when they were literally the only people I knew outside of Hound.

"Yeah, okay. Close your eyes, Laura."

I crinkled my brow. What? Why couldn't I watch? Was this some sort of magic trick? They'd shifted yesterday in plain view.

Noah read my expression again and giggled. "I mean, hell, you can keep your eyes open if you want. Most hybrid shifters like us don't give a shit about nudity, but I wasn't certain if you were quite there yet."

My cheeks flamed. *Duh. Right.* They possibly had to take off their clothes to shift, and Noah was just trying to make sure I was comfortable.

I swallowed hard. Part of me wished he hadn't said anything at all, because now that he'd warned me, I really felt like I *should* close my eyes.

But if I was totally truthful to myself? I didn't want to.

Because I want to watch the shift happen, my inner voice argued unpersuasively. *I just want to see how it works. That's all.*

It had totally nothing to do with pondering what their tanned skin and defined muscles looked like when they weren't covered up with clothes. Or wondering what their—

Oh Jesus.

Praying my face wasn't as red as it felt, I squeezed my eyes shut. I heard a giggle that I was pretty sure came from Jack, and then rustling sounds as the two men removed their clothes. Even though I couldn't see them, I swore the atmosphere in the room changed the second they were undressed. As if it became charged with some kind of low-level electricity.

Goose bumps grew out on my skin, and my breath fastened.

Then another noise filled the space. A sort of whooshing, cracking sound. I waited for one of them to tell me I could look, only realizing how silly that was when a cold hand touched my hand.

My eyes flew open, and I looked down at the two huge shifters. They stood on either side of the bed, and they looked so odd in the seedy hotel room that I almost giggled. Both of them had stark dark fur, and one had his black nose pressed to my hand. His nose was cold and wet, but his breath was hot.

As I looked down, his large pink tongue swiped out to lick my hand. I let out a surprised sound that was half gasp, half laugh.

They were beautiful.

Striking.

Incredible.

Tentatively, I scooted off the end of the bed, my gaze darting back and forth between the two huge shifters. They padded toward me, meeting me as I stood up. My heart thundered in my chest, but shockingly, I wasn't afraid. I stretched out my hand, and the vampire shifter on my right moved closer, allowing me to stroke the soft, thick hair on his back.

I swore I felt him shiver under my touch, and he must've loved it, because he pressed closer to me. I stroked his ears, they were soft as silk underneath my fingertips.

A low shriek sounded to my left, bringing a smile to my face.

"I haven't forgotten about you," I answered, as I turned to the other shift—which, according to where the guys had been standing when they shifted, should be Jack. He moved closer to me as his lips drew back in what was almost a smile. Leaving one hand on Noah, I scratched Jack's shift behind the ear as he leaned into my touch.

This was unbelievable. I felt like Snow White or something, able to control with the wild animals of the forest.

Except these weren't *just* animals. Beneath that, they were also men.

Men I was currently stroking shamelessly. Not that either of them appeared to mind one bit.

But the astonishing thing was, that realization didn't make me blush. Any uneasiness or clumsiness I felt around them when they were human melted away when they were in their shift forms. And oddly, I felt more certain I could trust them now than ever. There was something so pure about them in this form. Not "pure" as in angelic—Jack's shift had the same wicked spark in his eyes as the man himself did—but rather, something primal. Basic. Something that existed in black and white, with none of the messy shades of grey humans were made of.

It made a pleasing shiver run up my spine, and I knelt on the floor, allowing the large shifters to press closer to me. Each shift's eyes reflected their human features. Jack's were dark amber and Noah's were an icy grey. Both sets of eyes watched me keenly, but this time, I didn't feel like prey.

I felt strong. Powerful.

"You're beautiful," I muttered, running my soft warm fingers through the thick hair of Noah's shift.

His large head whirled toward mine, leaving our noses barely an inch apart. I could hear the soft *whiffs* of his breath, and the eyes that stared into mine were bright with intelligence.

I stared into them, lost in their blue depths and unconcerned in ever finding my way back.

Then his soft hair tickled my face, and the spell broke as a belly laugh burst forth from my throat. I rested back against the foot of the bed, laughing and wriggling, as the hybrid shifts wagged their tails, gathering around me to rub me all over.

With no warning, the door burst open.

Norman stepped halfway inside, his hand fixed on the handle. He was breathing heavily, and at the sight of me on the floor with two of his clutch mates, he stopped, his eyes widening slightly. Then he shook off whatever reaction he'd had, his gaze snapping into focus.

"We've got company. We got to go. *Now!*"

Chapter 13-Vampire on the Run

Fear soured my stomach at the urgency in his tone.

He sprinted into the room, seizing one of the backpacks and drawing a gun from inside it. Then he flicked the safety off and stalked back to the door, cracking it open to peer down into the parking lot.

The two vampire hybrid shifters prowled away from me, their hairs rising.

Swallowing down my fear, I grabbed for the backpack on the bed, but Norman's hiss pulled my attention. I looked up at him, and he shook his head.

"Leave it, Laura. We'll get other clothes. Get behind me. Get prepared to run."

I let go of the strap, getting off the bed and padding over to stand behind Jack. The breadth of his shoulders mostly obstructed my view out the door, but I felt safer behind the muscled man than almost anywhere else.

"Three men. Armed. The blond Terminator is definitely the leader. Two are in the office, one outside."

Norman rattled off the information in a clipped tone. At first I supposed he was speaking to me, but then Jack's shift huffed a breath, and I realized Jack's report was probably for their benefit.

"Where's Marcus?" I whispered. "Did you guys steal a car?"

"Yeah."

Norman flashed me a look like he was shocked I was keeping my shit together. The truth was, my insides felt like ice water. But crying in a corner wouldn't get us out of here.

"The Hound hunters pulled into the parking lot right behind us, so he had to park on the far side." He jerked his chin. "He's got the engine running. We just need to get there."

"Okay." My throat went dry, and I could feel the tension everywhere.

Norman narrowed his eyes at me, his dark gaze assessing. "You ever shot a gun, Laura?"

"N-no."

He nodded decisively, then drew another handgun from the back of his waistband and shove it into my hands. "*Squeeze* the trigger, don't pull it. Shoot at anyone who tries to harm you."

The weapon felt like a brick of ice in my grip, cold and heavy. I wrapped both hands around it as the metallic taste of fright danced across my tongue. Norman used his gun to edge the door open a little wider, looking in the direction of the office.

"Go! Now!"

His harsh whisper almost made me jump out of my skin, but my body impulsively obeyed his order. He threw the door open, and I was hot on his heels as he ran down the raised walkway that fronted the second story rooms. The two wolves raced behind me, their padded feet almost silent on the concrete slab. Just as we were about to reach the stairs that led down to the ground floor, shots rang out.

There was a loud metallic ping as one of the bullets ricocheted off the balcony's steel railing. I screamed and ducked, raising my arms to cover my head as best I could. I still gripped the gun, and I could feel the grip slipping between my sweaty palms.

"Back! Go back!"

Norman screeched to a stop and pointed behind him as a man in a black shirt and fatigues rounded the stairs. The man raised his gun, but before he could shoot, Norman fired several rounds at him.

And then we were running again, back the way we came. This time the shifts were in front, and I could feel Norman close on my heels, guarding my body with his own. Heavy footsteps sounded behind us, and Norman wrapped an arm around me, pinning me to the side of the building with his massive frame while he raised his right arm and shot at our pursuer.

A pained cry rose up, but before I could look to see what had happened to the man, Norman pulled me away from the wall, shoving me forward. I stumbled as I ran, but managed to keep my feet. The second level balcony wrapped all the way around the building, and we turned the corner at a sprint. Another set of stairs led down on this side, and I put on an extra burst of speed when I saw them.

Whoever had been behind us had been slowed down — maybe stopped — by Norman's shots. But there were still two more men unaccounted for.

Jack and Noah loped down the steps ahead of me. The old staircase rattled and shook as I ran after them.

But before Norman could join us, the huge, blond, scary-as-fuck man rounded the corner on the second level, coming from the back of the hotel. He broke into a graceful, powerful run, bearing down on the vampire shifter like a runaway train. Norman fired at him, but the bullet went wide, barely slowing him down at all.

Shit!

As I turned around and started to run back up the stairs, something dragged me to a stop. When I looked back over my shoulder, Noah's shift had his jaws fastened to the back of my t-shirt.

"No! We have to help him! Let go!"

Norman and the Terminator were trading fire on the second level, and every echoing gunshot made my stomach turn to ice. In the distance, I was vaguely aware of sirens wailing. Someone in the hotel must've called the cops.

Noah's shift gray eyes flashed, and if he could've spoken, I was sure he'd say something like, "Let *us* aid him, you dummy."

Jack's shift form raced up the steps past me as Noah pulled me backward. I slipped down a step, my movements clumsy and awkward, before I finally yielded and turned around to run on my own. An engine revved, and tires screeched as Marcus whipped the stolen car through the parking lot, driving as close to our side of the building as possible.

The shift beside me howled, urging me on faster. I ran toward the burgundy Honda, my breath coming in short gasps. But as we drew near to it, a figure stepped around the side of the building.

The third man.

He wore a dark shirt and cargo pants like his colleagues, but my brain barely registered that fact. It was too focused on the gun he held in his hand.

A wave of emotions rushed through me. Images of my Father flashed through my mind. Of the way he'd stood—his feet braced, his shoulders squared. Of the look on his face as he aimed and fired at me.

The new man raised his gun, and I pulled up my own weapon at the same time, pointing it at his chest. Only a few yards separated us. At this distance, even an amateur marksman like me had a good chance of hitting their target.

But my finger resting on the trigger wouldn't move. It felt stuck, as if my hand—hell, maybe my entire body—belonged to someone else. My arm shook. All I could look at was the shiny black barrel of his gun. All I could hear was my Father's voice, rushing in my ears in a stream of whispered promises and lies.

The man smirked, reading my expression and recognising his victory. His trigger finger twitched as he took a half-step forward.

But before his foot hit the ground, a flash of white raced past me.

A shot rang out, and a splash of red stained the shift's snowy fur as he pounced on the man.

The two of them went down heavily. The shift's sharp claws pinned the man's shoulders as he growled down at our attacker. The man tried to leverage his arm up to get another clear shot, but in a flash, sharp fangs closed around his neck.

A harsh, gurgling cry echoed in the air before cutting off abruptly. The shift's fangs snapped together loudly as he tore out the man's throat. Blood sprayed, large droplets raining over the dirty cement. Some of it hit me, warm and wet.

I froze, gazing at the man in the cargo pants and the shift standing over him. The shift's white snout and black nose were covered in blood, the red so bright it almost looked unreal.

Another shot rang out, and my body jerked. I ducked instinctively, throwing my hands over my head.

"Move!" Norman yelled from behind us.

He and the other white shift raced down the stairs from the second level. They both sprinted flat out, overtaking us in a few seconds. Jack shifted as he ran, barely breaking pace as he changed from his shift back into a man. I hardly had a chance to register the fact that he was naked before a hand locked onto my arm, pulling me toward the car. Noah shoved me roughly inside, diving in after me. Jack leapt in after him and Norman forced open the front passenger door, slamming his hand down on the dash.

"Go, go, go!"

Marcus was already peeling out, driving over the curb as he turned the car sharply and drove toward the main road. Norman leaned out the window and fired behind us, catching the blond Terminator in the shoulder as he raced across the parking lot. The man spun sideways, his momentum thrown off. He held tight his arm and straightened, glaring after us.

"I shot him." Norman pulled back inside the window, resting back into the seat and keeping an eye on the rear-view mirror. "And his other compatriots are dead. Get us quickly out of here, Marcus."

"On it."

Trees whipped by as Marcus rode the accelerator hard, driving us out of town.

My heart drummed so hard I swore it rattled my rib cage. I clutched the edge of the seat, turning to face the two naked men who sat in the back with me. They were both breathing hard too, their powerful, muscled chests rising and falling. Jack had a light dusting of hair across his chest, while Noah's was smooth. Their abs contracted with each harsh breath, and a sheen of sweat covered their skin.

And Noah...

I forced my gaze up from his body to his face, and my stomach tightened. The lower half of his face was wet with blood. It dripped down his chin, splitting into small pink rivulets when it met with the sweat on his chest. The blood-covered muzzle had been disconcerting on his beautiful white shift form, but the effect now was truly chilling.

He looked wild. Bloodthirsty.

My stare must not have been subtle, because he glanced down at me. His grey-blue eyes shuttered, the first time I'd ever seen them be anything but open and warm. Jack dug into one of the packs placed on the floor by the front seat before throwing a piece of cloth back at Noah.

Noah snatched it out of the air silently and used it to wipe away the blood that laid on his face. A slightly pinkish tinge remained, but at least he didn't look like untamed anymore.

He threw the rag back up to Jack, exchanging the bloodied cloth for a change of clothes. Norman handed Jack some clothes too, and the two men awkwardly slipped them on. I tried not to glare, but in the tiny confinement of the car, there was barely anywhere else *to* look.

"You okay, Laura?" Noah asked softly, lifting his butt to slide his pants up.

He was going commando, I realized. Jack had only given him pants and a shirt. As soon as he tucked himself away and drew the zipper up, I was able to breathe again.

But that breath stuttered in my chest when I tried to answer him. Leftover adrenaline made me shake. I looked up into Noah's soft, sweet eyes, unable to comprehend that less than ten minutes ago, he'd killed a man. Murdered him in one of the most vicious ways possible.

And he'd done it to save me.

I nodded shakily. "Yes. I'm sorry. I should've shot him. I tried to, but I—"

"You aren't a killer." He dropped the shirt he was about to pull over his head, stretching out his hands to tuck a Hound of hair behind my ears. "You shouldn't be embarrassed of that, Laura. That's a good thing. We do what we have to to thrive. But what this world has turned me into? I'm not always proud of it."

"Pride and survival don't always go hand in hand," Jack added, darkness clouding his usually cheery voice.

For a minute, I let myself be stupid and give in to my impulse. I leaned into Noah's touch, letting the tips of his fingers skim my cheekbones as his large palm cradled my chin.

I shouldn't be turning to him for comfort. Not when he was also the same wild beast who'd scared me. But my body didn't seem to realize that. It craved his strength and power, the safety he could offer in an unsafe world I wasn't equipped to survive on my own.

Reaching up, I pulled Noah's forearm—whether to push him away or pull him closer, I wasn't sure. His eyes locked with mine, and the fingers brushing the side of my face slipped over to tangle in my hair.

He'd missed a spot with the towel. A smear of blood stained one of his cheeks, and my gaze zeroed in on it, trying to reconcile the two sides of him.

I'd seen the beauty of his shift. And I'd seen the ugliness of it.

Both sides existed inside this sweet, caring man.

"Fuck. Hound isn't joking around."

Norman's voice from the front seat drew our attention, and Noah finally pulled his hand away, slipping his shirt over his head. As he did, I noticed the red line along his ribs leaking slow droplets of blood.

Oh shit. The bullet the man had fired as Noah leapt for him. It'd just grazed his side, but another inch or two to the right and...

Dread welled up in my chest, and I forced myself not to finish that thought, focusing on the discussion going on around me.

"Hound never jokes around. They want to kill us for breaching into their fucking facility, and they want *her*" — Marcus's bright blue eyes stared at me through the rear-view mirror — "back."

"That blond asshole is named Jason. I heard his buddy call him that. And he's a fucking lap dog. I'm sure of it." Jack's lip curled.

"Did you see him shift?" Marcus asked sharply, moving his gaze away from me.

"Nah. I bet he's under orders not to in case of eyewitnesses. But I would bet my brother's life on it."

"What's a... a lap dog?" I asked.

Jack shook his head in disgust. He still hadn't put his shirt on, and the muscles of his arms bunched as he pressed his fists together. "Almost every test subject in the Hound Facility's shifter initiative was brought in against their will. Kids stolen from the foster system, homeless people taken off the street. But there are a select few who volunteered. Who gave up their human lives to become enforcers for Hound. Ex-military, mercenary types, mostly."

"And the Terminator guy—he's one of those? He's a shifter too?"

"Yeah. Which makes him dangerous as fuck."

I trembled, picturing the big, thick-necked man. All the guys in the car with me were big, but he towered over even them. And if he could shift too? What must his shift look like? What would it be capable of?

"How did they know where we were? How did they find us so quickly?" I looked out the rear window again, watching the highway disappear into the distance. I half expected to see Jason back there, gunning for us, but we'd left him behind. For the moment, at least.

"I don't know," Noah said softly. "Maybe they put out an alert for us. Maybe they're doing a broader sweep than we thought."

"The clerk could've reported us. He was glaring at Laura, and when I shut that shit down, he got testy."

Jack glanced back at me, and I remembered how he'd wrapped his arms around me possessively. Recalled the anger in the desk clerk's eyes. Would he really have called the cops out of spite?

Then I recollected the way the grungy man's lip had curled when he looked at Jack, and my stomach twisted. Yeah, he probably would have. And even though they hadn't come, if the Hound lap dog was monitoring police radios, he'd have heard it called in.

How could people be so awful?

I pulled my legs up to my chest, wrapping my shaking arms around my knees.

"It doesn't matter how they fucking found us. It matters that they did. And we can't let it happen again." Marcus scowled. "We need to ditch this car fast."

Chapter 14 -Captured

I had expected Marcus to pull over immediately after making that dire statement. But instead, we drove a while longer, as tension filled the atmosphere in the van.

As Noah pointed out to me in a low voice if I was truly the prized experiment they all thought I was, Hound would want me alive. And with the help of his lap dogs the lives of the four guys I now had as family was in grave danger.

So, definitely bad news.

Noah's words triggered thoughts flowing through my head, how my live could cost the lives of them all, this made my spine ache since they were now the closest I had to family. But as if he had been reading my thoughts he placed his hands on my thighs, his gaze fixed on mine as he let out one of those devastating smiles he had which stood on his broad face, smiles that cared less about the taste of death. Smiles that laid on the face that hours ago had almost taken a bullet for me.

"Where are we?" I questioned, sitting up and stretching my cramped muscles as I looked out the windows. The scenery had changed, becoming more sparse and desert-like. Marcus slowed the car as we pulled into a small roadside rest area.

"New Mexico," he said shortly.

I catalogued everything I saw, fascinated in spite of myself. We passed by a fast food place, and I had to fight the urge to press my face to the glass like a two-year-old. I was starving. Those donuts had been all I had taken hours ago.

Marcus pulled into a dingy gas station and we piled out of the car and split up as.

Norman and Noah took me to McDonalds and watched in awe as I stared up at the menu. They finally ordered what looked like one of everything on the menu.

As Noah paid in cash, Norman glanced out the large front windows.

"Here we go," he muttered.

I followed his gaze, my heart beating in fear. Was Jason here? Had he found us again already?

The sight of the broad shoulder lap dog rattled my heart in its rib cage. My stomach began to growl in hunger and pain, we had just evaded an attack few hours ago by a hairs breath and now we were faced with another immediately.

"How did he follow us" looking up at Jack I probed. With his gaze still fixed on the terminator blond he shook his head, disbelief written all over his face.

We had caught the attention of Noah, who at the sight of Jason pulled me behind him with his left hand. I held on to his hands behind him as fear shivered through my body, the sight of Jason had brought out the fright I thought I had locked deep down. "What next?" "What do we do now?" questions kept pouring through my frightened mind.

Marcus and Norman had just driven into the filing station a large grey minivan when Jason's gaze met Normans

"Fuck"

"Reverse......drive back"

Norman shouted as Marcus jammed the brakes, his hands on the wheels and his eyes on the road reversing from Jason who rained shots on the minivan as Marcus made a race for the road.

"Take Laura away from here" pulling the cold metallic gun from the pack he carried on his shoulders. Noah responded almost immediately his grip on my hands still tight

"Find somewhere to hide" gesturing to the lady at the counter who stood frozen in fear at the sound of gunshots. His grip still glued firmly to my hands as we both raced for the back door, bending our head to the waist level.

Jack raced out the complex raining shots at the broad shouldered blond, who followed Marcus and Norman with a range of shots as the minivan pulled back to the road. His first shot went wide but the second caught the blond by the leg throwing him to the ground in anger and pain.

With his gun still held firmly in his hand, he walked towards Jason sending another shot to the wounded lap dog that let out a shout of pain as the bullets pierced through his skin.

Noah had taken Laura through the back door, his eyes fixed on the road watching out for any other threat to their lives. Taking a number of turns as they raced to safety with nowhere in mind just far away from the sight of Jason, Noah's grip tightened the longer the distance we covered. I was about to let go of his hands when another round of shot pierced the air, his grip tightened as we raced with an extra burst of speed.

Jason laid on the floor in pain his hands holding on to his wounded legs as he struggled to get on his feet

"You're not that tough after all" pushing him back to the ground Jack grinned, holding firm to the trigger of his gun.

A shot broke into the air

Jack let go of the trigger slowly turning around in to see who had shot him at the back piercing through his chest releasing blood slowly from his mouth. His gaze met a dozen more compatriots of Jason, he had called for reinforcements immediately he was sure the four shifters were at the filing station.

Two more shots filled the air, one piercing through his heart and the other perfecting the damage as it passed through his heart. Jack dropped dead his eyes wide open as blood flowed from his body to the concrete floors of the filing station.

"Take care of the body" Jason struggled to get back on his feet placing both hands on the floor to strengthen his wounded leg

"They still got the project and they have not gotten far for our chase" Jason with his hands on the neck of two his compatriots as they led him to the vehicle they parked by the road. Limping he managed to fit his body into the car pulling out a gun from the bag that laid quietly at the back seat of the car.

We had just run some miles that I had not run for a long time. The last time my body felt this way was back at the training session after my attack when Ernie had put me through a couple of drills. But this was no training drill, I was running for my life and though we had raced far on our own loosing sight of Jason and his compatriots my heart still rattled within and I deep down I still felt I had to run.

Noah leaned on the wall his head towards the sky as we both were breathing heavily. The thought of the safety of his brothers crossed his mind and now he had began to doubt the fact that they were still alive, he had heard a couple of shots as he and Laura ran on the streets and guessed that to be Jacks but the range of shots that had later pierced the air and the deadly silence after that built a castle of doubt on his sweaty face.

We had just stopped running and had barely had few minutes to catch our breaths when the sound of sirens echoed in the distance. Noah could guess from the sound of the sirens that there were a couple of backups that had come with Jason and almost immediately as he heard the sound, he sprung to his feet pulling my weak body by my hands, but my feet wobbled in disagreement.

"Do we have to keep running?" I gave him a querying look as I pointed to my trembling feet

"Yes, we have Laura" Kneeling by my side as his warm hands lifted my face to his. I wondered within myself how he still had the touch of love amidst the chaos, his hands on my cheek had released a bit of fear that lurked hidden within. I looked into his eyes resting my cheekbone on his strong warm hands, the temptation to place my lips on his beautiful lips grew strong and so to avoid that I decided to close my eyes. The battle to resist was not only my battle as Noah gracefully let his eyes gaze down at my body and back to my lips where he lost the fight as he moved closer sinking his lips in mine.

"A kiss"

It was my very first and it felt so good locking lips with Noah as his body pressed against mine a little closer.

The blaring noise of the siren that echoed in the air brought us back to the chaos, we stopped pulling away our lips. Noah took me by the waist and carried me over his shoulders and we continued our run.

Oh, how I hated Hound he had wrecked my life and now had wrecked my first kiss. His lips felt so warm, I could feel the purity in his heart as our lips met, it felt so odd and basically so romantic that I was having my first kiss at this age of my life and so romantic that it had to come amidst the chaos. Who would have thought that love still had a room for me---I guess everyone, if I don't concentrate and focus more on escaping from Hound and his world.

We had not run far before a minivan pulled up front, Noah stopped for a split second and seemed to race down towards it. It was Marcus and Norman; the blaring of the sirens had been their blue print to get to us and luckily for us we had outsmarted Jason for the second time------ at least we thought we had.

Noah let me down carrying me into the van as he hurried into it as the sirens now blared closer and a range of shots began to ring out. Marcus stepped on the accelerator making a tur for the road when.........

Marcus had barely enough time to look at his side mirrors as he made a turn for the road, just when I thought we were out of the grip of Hound and its schemes, when I thought love had granted me an opportunity, Jason crushed it.

Jason riding a truck came out of the blue has he sped towards us, we all had little time to see him before the truck hit the van hard sending us down a steep into the woods that was beside the road.

Rolling and tumbling, I could feel my body tearing within me. I could hardly hear my screams as we rolled down the steep and down into flames.

Tears rolled down my eyes as I felt the heat of the flames rising, blood raced down the windows of the van. Noah held my hands and tears rolled down his eyes, we all wanted freedom, to live life the way humans lived before we were taken by Hound.

"Sir, its done" Jason said as he watched from the truck the minivan go in flames.

THE END

Lightning Source UK Ltd.
Milton Keynes UK
UKHW020644240521
384271UK00011B/741